Utopia, Texas

A Novel By Joe Totten

Cover design by **Brian Danaher**

Interior design by **Devin Sharp**

First Edition

Printed in the United States of America

ISBN (Paperback): 978-1- 7329925-4-2

ISBN (Kindle): 978-1-7329925-5-9

Library of Congress Control Number: 202690664

For permissions or inquiries:

Joe Totten

jtotten99@gmail.com

For Maria, Lucy, Ben, and Sammy. Lots of love.

1

He stood in the kitchen, hands on his hips, back straight, looking out at the lawn I'd forgotten to mow. His posture suggested he was about to receive an order or give one. My father always stood at attention, which made sense after twenty-five years in the army.

"You're driving Rue to Texas," he said. "She wants to go to a funeral."

I nodded and didn't ask who died, not that I wasn't interested. I just didn't want to prolong the conversation any longer than necessary.

"You'll leave tomorrow after school," he said and walked out of the kitchen.

Her full name is La Rue Audrey Birdwell, but everyone calls her Rue. I never called her grandmother. She hated the word. There's nothing grand about getting old, she'd say. I barely knew my grandfather, Calvin, her husband of more than thirty years. Rue rarely talked about him. A small picture frame next to her bed held the only photo of him in her home. Calvin is standing in a rowboat, waving his hat at the camera. Rue is seated at the oars. She doesn't look happy.

According to my father, Calvin was a man of unchangeable habits. He wanted his dinner on the table every evening at six sharp, his son out of sight, and his wife quiet. That last one was impossible for Rue, and the marriage became a battle. Everyone was forced to pick a side. My dad chose Rue, and now I'm stuck with her.

Later that afternoon, I rode my bike over to Rue's house. Her 1963 Coupe DeVille Cadillac was in her carport, covered in dust. Despite numerous dents in the side panels and a thick coat of dust, this was a beautiful car. Baby blue with a white leather interior. I could lie down in the back seat, and my head and feet wouldn't touch either door. Sharp, chrome-trimmed tailfins sweeping back from the rear window gave the impression the car might go airborne any second. The steering wheel is as big as a manhole cover. There was enough metal on that Cadillac for two small cars. The last time Rue had been at the wheel, she wiped out a few trash cans wheeling out of the church parking lot, and my old man had taken the keys from her.

This time of day, she'd be in front of the TV watching her soaps with the volume up so loud the dishes rattled. I knocked and waited. After a few minutes, the door opened as far as the chain would allow. The old lady's face floated into view.

"It's Jim," I said.

I could hear her swearing, trying to get the chain loose, then the door swung wide.

"Have you got the keys, boy?"

I showed her the keys. "Dad says we'll leave tomorrow after I get home from school."

She shook her head. "I want to get an early start. We've got a ways to go."

"I got school tomorrow, Rue."

"School? Don't bother. It's not doing you any good."

When the phone rang the next morning, it was still dark. My room was closest to the kitchen, where the phone hung on the wall, so it was assumed that I would answer it. I picked up the receiver.

It was Rue. "We're wasting daylight, boy. Let's go."

We took the interstate, heading west toward Atlanta. In the rush to get out of the house, I'd forgotten to bring a road map.

"We don't need a map," Rue said. "I know where I'm going."

Northern Georgia is a monotonous landscape of thick stands of pine trees and wide fields of cotton behind miles of wire fence. I turned on the radio. The Supremes singing *Love Child* came on. Rue listened for a while and then snapped off the radio.

"Hey, I was listening to that."

"I'm not listening to those people screaming at me."

I looked at her. "What do you mean by those people?"

She turned her head and stared out the window. "What word do we use nowadays...Negro, colored?"

"Black or African American."

"I've been calling 'em something else my whole life. I'm not changing now."

"Rue, that word is offensive. Please don't use it."

"Know what offends me, smart guy? When those people burn down their own homes, then expect the government to bail them out."

"What are you talking about?"

She turned to look at me. Rue wore thick glasses that made her eyes appear oddly large.

"I was struck by lightning when I was a child," she said, trying to change the subject.

That explains a lot, I thought.

"There was a pecan tree next to our house, with a rope hanging from one of the limbs. My younger brother and I…"

"You mean Uncle Percy?"

"Stop interrupting, boy. I'm telling a story."

"Yes, ma'am."

"Well…I was standing under the tree, and Percy was standing at the corner of the house next to the rain barrel. Mother was at the screen door looking at the sky. I have never seen a sky look like that, before or since. Dark. Boiling. God's angriest face. Suddenly, this silver finger came down and touched the top of the tin roof. Traveled across the tin, down the drain pipe, jumped onto Percy, and then skipped over to where I was standing. By the time the lightning hit me, it must have run out of steam. All I felt was a light shiver. Felt cold and hot at the same time.

"The lightning knocked Percy to the ground. Mother and I ran to him. His eyes were open, and he was breathing, but he couldn't move. Mother carried him to the house and laid him on his bed. He didn't eat or drink or say a word for three days. Our beds were so close I could reach out and touch him. For those days, I wasn't sure it was Percy lying in that bed or some evil phantom. I thought God had taken his soul and left his body behind. There are things in this world beyond our understanding, boy. You can deny it all you want, but it just shows your ignorance. I would wake up in the night and look over at him. His eyes were wide open, arms stiff at his side. I thought about holding a pillow over his face, finishing the job God had started. I didn't want him trapped in a useless body, stuck somewhere between Heaven and Texas. Percy never closed his eyes the whole time, just stared out into the dark, his chest moving slowly up and down.

"One morning, I opened my eyes, and Percy was sitting up in his bed, smiling at me. Said he could smell the bacon Mother was cooking for breakfast. He ate like he had a hollow leg, and when he was finished, Mother asked him where he'd been for the past three days. Said he didn't know, but it sure wasn't Utopia, Texas. He didn't do much the rest of that summer. Spent a lot of time on the porch, reading. Which was strange for him; he'd never liked books before. Now he read everything: the newspaper, the Bible, the Sears and Roebuck catalogue. He even read the repair manual for the International Harvester. Unless the sky was blue and fair, I couldn't get him to play with me out in the yard. And he was deathly afraid of clouds.

"I need to use the ladies' room. Find me a filling station and pull over."

"What happened to Percy?"

Rue looked at me. "What do you mean?"

"Why does he live in California and not Texas?"

"Ever been to California, boy?"

"No ma'am."

"Didn't think so. If you'd ever been, you would not ask such a stupid question."

2

I pulled into a gas station and parked. Rue climbed out slowly and walked inside. I turned on the radio. There was news about the Apollo mission. There had been an explosion in the capsule. The announcer said the astronauts were more than a hundred thousand miles from Earth, and it wasn't clear if they could make it back with the oxygen they had onboard.

I opened the glove box and took out the letter I had brought from home. It looked very official, a government seal stamped in the upper corner of the envelope. I was afraid to open it, so I stuffed it back in the glove box.

Watching Rue walk across the gravel lot and climb in the car, I realized she moved pretty well for an eighty-year-old woman.

"I just saw the ugliest man I think I've ever seen," she said. "He was standing behind the counter. Big jug ears and a nose like a cooked sausage. I wonder what ugly people do when it comes to marriage? I suppose they find other ugly people to love. That would explain all the awful-looking folks wandering around this state. And most of them hold public office."

I ignored her. She was always going off on strangers.

"Are you getting hungry?"

"I'll tell you when I'm hungry," she snapped. "Let's go."

I put the car in gear and eased onto the highway. Rue leaned back and closed her eyes.

"Would you please put on your seat belt?" I said.

She looked at me. "Who the hell are you, Ralph Nader?"

"If we have an accident…"

"Look, sonny boy, what I do in the privacy of my own vehicle is none of the government's goddam business."

If I were going to be stuck in the car with her for two days, I needed to relax and not let her get to me.

She leaned against the door, closed her eyes, and was asleep in minutes, mouth open, breathing loudly. I looked over at her. My father told me she used to have light brown hair, but when her husband died, her hair turned white almost overnight.

The sky had suddenly gone dark, gray clouds crowding out the blue. The Caddy bounced over a rough spot in the road, shaking Rue awake. "Where are we?"

"Just crossed into Alabama."

"There's a good chicken joint up ahead. How about we have our dinner?"

Rue waited in the car while I stood at the window. A large, smiling Black woman took our order. Two plate lunches with white meat, fried okra, and cornbread. And two sweet teas.

"That should be out in a minute, hon," the woman said.

A storm was coming. Pine trees lining the highway swayed in the strong wind. The low clouds were tight over the green landscape.

3

The weather finally caught up with us just outside Birmingham. In minutes, the road was flooded, and the rain came down in sheets, rolling across the asphalt. I could feel the Caddy slipping on the slick surface, so I pulled onto the shoulder and turned off the windshield wipers. Rue had fallen asleep again. I wanted to turn on the radio for a weather report, but I was afraid it would wake her. So I just sat there watching the water stream down the windows, listening to the rain drumming on the roof.

My graduation was in a few weeks, and my old man had told me I had only two choices: get a job and start paying rent, or go to college. I was pretty sure those weren't my only options, but I wasn't going to argue with him. I looked at Rue, head against the window, mouth open, and wondered how much of her craziness I'd inherited. Mother and son couldn't have been more different. My father was all about the rules, while Rue was always pushing back, determined to get her own way, regardless of what anyone else thought.

The rain stopped, the clouds moved on, and the sun came out. The road was dry in minutes, steam drifting up from the pavement. We cruised through dense stands of pine, past red dirt farm roads intersecting the highway. Very little traffic. Up ahead, I saw a car parked on the shoulder of the highway with the hood up. A young woman leaned against the fender, smoking a cigarette. She looked harmless, with faded jeans, a gray sweatshirt with the sleeves cut short, and a small leather bag. I slowed down and eased the Caddy up behind her car. She threw down the cigarette and walked over.

"Car trouble?" I said.

"How'd you guess?"

"Can we give you a ride somewhere?"

She yawned and stretched. "Sure, why not?" She leaned over and looked inside the Caddy. "Where are you taking Granny?"

Before I could answer, she opened the back door and climbed in. When she pulled the door shut, Rue opened her eyes. We were back on the highway before Rue noticed someone in the back seat.

Rue turned her head. "Who is this woman?"

"Don't worry about it, Granny. Go back to sleep."

"Her car broke down," I said. "We're giving her a ride."

Rue shook her head. "Not in my car, we're not."

The woman leaned forward. "The Christian thing to do would be to help a stranded traveler." "What's your name, young lady?"

"Milly. What's yours?"

"Does your Mother know you're out here on the highway accepting rides from strangers?"

Milly laughed. "Momma gave up years ago."

We rode in silence for miles, passing small farms with faded barns, cows standing in green pastures, dusty, rundown houses set back in the trees. Rusty pickups are parked in the front yard.

"There's a gas station up here," I said. "You can call someone."

I turned to look at Milly. She was holding a pistol pointed at the back of Rue's head.

She smiled at me. "There's no one to call."

My heart was pounding. I tried not to panic. "I need gas, ok?"

She nodded.

I pulled off the highway and parked in front of a gas pump.

Over the door of the gas station was a hand-painted sign: Gas, Guns, Food, Ice, Liquor.

"Why don't you come inside with me?" Milly said.

"I think I'll stay in the car."

"No, I think you'll come inside."

I climbed out of the Caddy and followed her inside. It was a small store with a worn wooden floor, shelves crowded with dusty merchandise, and no air conditioning. A large ceiling fan rattled overhead. A thin older woman smoking a cigarette stood behind the counter, watching us suspiciously. I walked toward the drink cooler at the back of the store. Milly stood by the door, looking around.

"This place is pathetic," she said. "I bet you don't do two hundred dollars on a good day?" She looked at the woman behind the counter. "Cigarettes, beer, and soda pop, that's your business, right?"

"Can I help you with something?" the woman said.

Milly stepped to the counter, pulled the pistol from her jeans, and showed it to the woman. "I want you to give me all the cash."

The woman didn't move.

Milly waved the pistol in her face. "I'm in kind of a hurry."

The woman put her cigarette in her mouth and opened the register, scooping out bills and stuffing them in a paper bag. The heat and humidity seemed to slow everything down; nothing seemed real. Milly stood calmly at the counter, holding the gun, the noisy fan spinning overhead.

I walked to the front of the store and placed a Dr. Pepper and two quarters on the counter.

"This is for the soda," I said. "I'm not with her."

The woman took the cigarette from her mouth. "You both come in the same car."

"I know, I know. But I was just giving her a ride."

Milly stuffed the pistol in her jeans, reached into her bag, and pulled out a Polaroid camera. She pointed the camera at the old woman and said, "Smile." The camera buzzed, and a blank picture slid out. Milly grabbed the bag of money and pushed open the screen door, laughing.

We climbed in the Caddy. I handed Rue the Dr. Pepper and pulled out onto the highway.

The old woman was probably giving the cops our license number right now. Should we stay on the main highway? Or switch to back roads until we were out of the state? How much money was in the register?

Milly sat in the backseat, counting the bills. Rue turned to look at her. "Why are you still in my car?"

"Nobody picked up the phone at home, and your
grandson has kindly offered to give me a ride."

Rue looked at me. "He's pretty generous with things that don't belong to him."

"I'll chip in some gas money, how about that?"

"Fine," Rue said.

I turned off the main highway, heading south on a secondary road.

Milly looked up. "Where are you going?"

"I don't think it's safe to travel on the main highway. You know...considering."

"I mean, where are you and Granny going?"

"Her name is Rue. We're going to a funeral in Texas."

"Who died?"

I shook my head. "I don't know."

"You don't know? You're driving all the way to Texas, and you don't know who died?"

I looked over at Rue. She was staring out the window.

"Rue, whose funeral are we going to?"

She didn't answer. I reached out and put my hand on her arm. "Rue?"

She turned toward me, her eyes were wet and red. "What are you bothering me about, now?"

"Why are we going to Texas…who died?"

She took a deep breath and exhaled. "My brother Percy."

"Percy's dead? When did this happen? Nobody told me."

"If you participated in this family once in a while, you might learn something."

Milly leaned forward. "Were you and your brother close?"

Rue opened her purse and took out a tissue. "I want to live as long as absolutely necessary and not a second longer. That's what Percy told me when he came back from
Europe."

"He was in the war?" Milly said.

"Percy came home one day holding a newspaper, telling Mother he was going to join up and go to France. She said, " You'll do no such thing. He said he was eighteen years old, and there wasn't a thing she could do to stop him. Mother sat up with him all night, crying, carrying on, trying to convince him not to go.

"She'd quote the Bible to him. The nation will not take up the sword against the nation, nor will they train for war anymore. Percy would throw a verse right back in her face. Put on the full armor of God, so that you can take your stand against the devil's schemes. Didn't do any good. He left the next morning. Months later, we got a postcard from Le Havre, France. It was a picture of Percy in his new uniform. He had a cigarette in his mouth, and he was holding a wine bottle. I can feel you worrying from over here, he wrote. Love, Percy.

"That war was an ugly machine that couldn't be stopped. Mother would not read the paper about the battles, but I did, and I regret it to this day. Men dying by the truckload. Didn't help to know the numbers of the dead and the places they were dying. The Somme, Messines, Belleau Wood. It's been more than fifty years, and I'll never get those names out of my head.

"Percy never wrote his family one letter from France; all he sent were postcards, pictures of the Eiffel Tower, the Arc de Triomphe, and the Palace of Versailles. On the back, he'd write: Love, Percy. Or, thinking about you. Or, be home soon.

"No news is worse than getting bad news. No news gives your mind plenty of room to contrive all kinds of evil stories. We prayed every day and then doubled up on Sundays. Mother refused to look at his postcards, didn't want 'em in the house. I kept them all, still have 'em, somewhere. I would look at those grand palaces and fancy monuments, and the war started to make sense. Folks over there had something worth fighting over. Then I'd look out my bedroom window at the brown, dry fields outside, and I couldn't imagine anyone getting excited about fighting over it. That's the difference between France and Texas. Over there, they have more things that need protecting.

"Then the war was over. All we wanted to see was Percy walking up to the house. Mother would stand at the kitchen window for hours, trying to imagine her boy strolling up that road, a rucksack over his shoulder. Instead, we got the mailman delivering another postcard. This one had a picture of the Hôtel La Villa d'Estrées in Paris with a note on the back: You can reach me here. Love, Percy.

"Mother wrote a letter the next day to the United States Army asking why her son Percy Childress was not returning from France with the rest of the boys. We got an answer a few weeks later, but it wasn't the one we wanted. Your son has deserted the United States Army, it read, and is in violation of Military Code something, something. Mother sat at the kitchen table and wrote a letter to Percy at the Hôtel La Villa d'Estrées. The letter was pages long, but every word amounted to the same thing: When are you coming home to Texas? It was early spring, and the war had been over for months by then. A postcard arrived, with the same picture of the Hôtel La

Villa d'Estrées. On the back, in a very neat script, was this message: I'm not coming home until they build a bridge across the Atlantic Ocean. Love, Percy.

"Then he disappeared for a while. No postcards, no letters. I remember Mother shaking her finger at Daddy, telling him he better pack his bags, cause he was going over there to get her boy. My father was a quiet man; he rarely ever raised his voice, and he most always deferred to Mother. But on this occasion, he waited until she was quiet and then said, The boy has been to war, Alma, and he survived. If he wants to live his life in Europe and not Texas, that's his own damn business. That shut her up.

"The next thing we knew, Percy was enrolled at the University of Vienna, and then he went to medical school in Berlin. This was a few years before Hitler, and his bunch took over. By this time, Percy was writing us postcards whenever something happened in his life. A train trip to Spain, a few days at the beach, a new apartment. Then, a few days before Christmas 1928, we got a letter and a picture. We hadn't seen a picture of Percy in almost ten years. There he was, standing in a park, wearing a black Homburg and a thick beard. He had his arms around a young woman. On the back of the photo, he'd written a note: Treptower Park, June 1928. Percy and Marta. The letter said that he and Marta were married that summer.

"Those were hard years in Texas; the rains never came, and we had to sell some of our land. Without Percy to help out, the work fell on Daddy. Then one day, we got a letter in a beautiful green envelope with our address on the front in an elegant script. It was from Marta. She tells us all about herself, her family, and where they live. They are Jewish. When Mother reads that part of the letter, she sets the pages on the table, goes outside, and sits on the porch for a long time. Our family follows the Seventh-day Adventists. Very inflexible people. No drinking, no dancing. They believe Jesus is coming back any day, and there is no sense in accumulating worldly possessions, as those things are useless in the afterlife.

"In her next letter, we find out that Marta's father owns a restaurant in Berlin and that she has two sisters. She tells us Percy, and she was working in the hospital. When Percy says hello, she knows he isn't German. She asks where he is from. Texas, he says. She asks if he was a cowboy. More like a plow boy, he replies. He tells her about his family in Texas, the farm he grew up on, and how he misses his parents and sister. But I don't miss Texas, he tells her, too hot and dry.

"We find out more about Percy than we have in years. He is happy in his new life. When he left home, he was eighteen, and we still thought about him as a boy. But now he is a grown man. Hearing about his life and how much of it we have missed makes us miss him even more. Marta writes that people are having a hard time. Prices keep going up, banks are closing, and everyone is very nervous about the political situation. But not to worry. Percy has a good job, we have a nice apartment, and we see my family often. One day we will all be together."

Rue turned to look out the window. "I'm tired now." Her voice was a little shaky. "I don't feel like talking anymore." She leaned back and closed her eyes.

4

The car was quiet for a long time. The Caddy rolled through a series of small Southern towns in the late afternoon. I don't remember the names, but they all had the same look. A single traffic light at the center of town, boarded-up storefronts, tractors parked on Main Street, old farmers standing in the shade. I glanced at Milly in the rearview mirror. She was looking out the window.

"Why did you take that woman's picture?"

She shrugged. "I like to take pictures."

"How much did you get?"

"Why do you care?"

"I don't know. I'm your driver. I thought maybe I should get something."

She laughed. "You forget who has the gun. You're not my partner, slick. You're an unwilling accomplice who might turn into a hostage if he doesn't shut the fuck up."

I turned on the radio. The news announcer said Apollo 13 was in trouble. The explosion in the main capsule's oxygen tank had forced the three astronauts to abandon the capsule and move into the lunar module. But the module only had enough oxygen for two days, and it would require four days for the spaceship and the astronauts to circle the moon and make it safely back to Earth.

"Those guys are in trouble," I said.

Milly laughed. "We're all in deep shit."

"What are you talking about?"

She leaned forward. "The Earth is a spaceship with four billion passengers. There's not enough food, water, or air for all of us. It's only a matter of time."

"Where do you live? I mean, where can I drop you?"

I looked at her smiling face in the rearview mirror. "I just decided. I'm going to Texas with you and Granny."

5

Late that afternoon, I found a small motor lodge, called 40 Winks, in the little town of Butler, Alabama. I parked in front of the office, went inside, and paid for one room. Two double beds, air conditioning, and a color TV, all for thirtytwo dollars a night. Rue was still asleep in the car. Milly climbed out of the Caddy, stretched, and wandered over to look at the pool.

I carried Rue's suitcase into the room, then gently woke her. She opened her eyes, uncertain for a few seconds, then sat up straight.

"Are you hungry?" I asked.

She grabbed her purse off the seat, opened it, and handed me a twenty.

"Go get me a pint of Johnnie Walker Black. And a pack of unfiltered Marlboros."

"I thought you quit smoking?"

"I did. Now I'm starting up again. What have I got to lose?"

Milly and I drove into town and found a liquor store. I was too young to buy liquor, so I handed her the twenty and asked her to buy the things Rue wanted.

She came back to the car with the Scotch, cigarettes, two pints of Bacardi, four packs of Slim Jims, and two Snickers bars.

"Where's the change?"

"What change?"

On the way back to the motel, we passed a large wooden building with a domed roof and a flashing sign out front: Carl's Skateland. The parking lot was full.

"Let's go give Granny her stuff," Milly said. "Then we're coming back here."

"I don't know how to skate."

She shook her head. "What kind of fucked up family did you come from?"

"My family's not fucked up…it was normal."

"Then how come you don't know how to skate?"

"I was doing other stuff…"

"Like what? Sitting in your room, playing with yourself?" I could feel my face turning red.

Milly smiled. "That's ok, Jimbo. It's never too late for a happy childhood."

When we got back to the room, Rue was sitting up in bed watching a baseball game with the sound off. I asked her if she wanted me to get her something to eat. She shook her head.

"Just get me one of those plastic cups from the bathroom."

She lit a cigarette, poured a drink, and took a long sip. "Jim, you're a lot like your father. You turn every little thing in life into a big worry."

That was the last thing I wanted to hear; the old man and I have something in common. "I just wanted to make sure you're ok, is all."

"You and your little friend run along. I'll be fine."

I parked outside the roller rink, and we went inside. The place was jammed.

While we were lacing up our skates, Milly handed me a pint of rum and told me to stuff it down my jeans and cover it with my shirt.

"What if I get caught?"

"Jesus Christ, what a pussy."

I barely knew this woman, but for some reason, I didn't want to disappoint her. I stuffed the bottle in my pants.

Milly rolled smoothly out onto the floor. I stood upright, moving cautiously out onto the wooden floor, staying close to the waist-high railing. Milly was already moving around the rink, dipping and turning through a mob of skaters, her arms over her head. A huge glitter ball spun from the ceiling, squares of light streaming across the walls and floor. *Mama Told Me Not to Come* was blasting out of the speakers. The music and the noise of the crowd echoed off the roof. Couples holding hands, kids screaming, people balancing on one skate. A young guy in cut-off jeans, skating backwards, zoomed past, a cigarette in his mouth. I stepped away from the railing and tried to get moving. Milly rolled up beside me and stopped.

"Like this," she said, "one foot pushes off, the other glides."

She coasted smoothly forward. I pushed off with one foot, getting a little glide.

"You got it."

She took my hand, pulling me onto the floor, dragging me around the rink. Our hands clamped together, picking up speed. The skaters' wheels made a deep rumbling sound on the wooden floor. Milly's dark hair was flowing behind her, her legs pumping. Then she let go of my hands. Struggling to keep my balance, I saw the railing ahead, but I didn't know how to stop or slow down. My skates hit the wall hard, and I flipped over the railing onto my back. I looked up, and Milly was standing at the railing, smiling.

"That wasn't funny."

"Yeah, it was."

She skated over to the snack bar and returned with cotton candy, popcorn, and hot dogs. We sat on a bench, watching the crowd.

"How many skaters are out there?" she said.

"Hard to count 'em. They're moving too fast."

"I'm guessing close to a hundred. And they all paid fifty cents to get in, plus a quarter for the skates, so…there's seventy-five bucks sitting in the office right now."

I looked at her. She pulled her hair into a ponytail.

"Don't even think about it."

"You're probably right. Too many witnesses and we're staying just down the road."

We finished our food, and Milly rolled out onto the floor, disappearing into the crowd of skaters. I moved out to the floor and, after several attempts, I was able to glide slowly along the railing, my legs working awkwardly. I saw Milly and the guy with the cut-off jeans holding hands, spinning tight circles at the center of the floor.

It was almost midnight when we drove back to the motel. Milly rolled down the window, letting the cool night air rush in. She opened the rum, took a long pull, and offered it to me. I shook my head.

I unlocked the door and stepped inside. The TV was still on, and Rue was asleep. Milly pushed past me and dropped her bag on the bed. "I'm gonna take a shower."

I turned off the TV, covered Rue with a blanket, and sat down on the empty bed. Milly's bag was on the bed. I wondered if the pistol was in there. I wasn't sure what I'd do with it, but knowing where it was seemed like a good idea. I opened her bag and dug around inside. A pack of Marlboros, a Bic lighter, the Polaroid camera, a paperback of *Steppenwolf*, a stack of pictures held together with a rubber band, and a

Tennessee driver's license with the name Millicent Fincher, date of birth March 27, 1949. The shower shut off, and I quickly stuffed everything back in her purse.

Milly stepped out of the bathroom in a T-shirt and underwear, the glare of light behind her. "You weren't going through my bag, were you?" I shook my head.

She sat down on the bed and took a sip from the rum. "I'm sleeping here. You're over there with Granny."

Milly was smiling, her hair was wet, and her face was pink. With her bare legs stretched across the bed and the bottle in her lap, she looked younger. We were only a few years apart, but there seemed to be many miles between us.

6

A few years ago, my father retired from the army after twenty-five years of service. He would have stayed in longer, but my Mother put her foot down and said, "No more." She was tired of moving every three years. Packing all our stuff, pulling my sister and me out of school, driving thousands of miles to a shitty little town outside an army base in Kansas or Oklahoma. Then, finding a house to rent, enrolling us in new schools, and getting to know new neighbors. Basically, starting our lives from scratch. All the old man has to do is put on his uniform, go to his new job, and assume that when he gets home, everything will be in order. That's how the army works. One soldier is the same as any other soldier, and one base looks like all the other bases. Families are just extra baggage.

In my twelve years of education, I attended eight different schools. I was always the new kid, the guy in the back of the classroom that nobody talked to because he showed up in the middle of the school year and looked out of place. And there was no good reason to get to know me. I wasn't good at sports, and I didn't play a musical instrument. I tried my best to fade into the background. My older sister, Nancy, had a different approach. She joined everything, Brownies, Girl Scouts, Candy Stripers, anything to fit in. I didn't care about fitting in because I knew I'd have to start all over again in a few years. Why bother?

I opened my eyes the next morning and looked around the room. The door was open, and Milly and Rue were gone. My first thought was they've taken the Caddy and left me in the middle of Alabama. I dressed quickly and stepped outside. Across the parking lot, in the shade of a tree, Milly and Rue were smoking cigarettes and talking. I walked over. Rue looked up and smiled.

"The look on this boy's face is always the same," she said to Milly, "like everything in the world is news to him."

We stopped for coffee and donuts, then headed west. It was a beautiful day. Cloudless blue skies, no wind, cool. It would get hotter as the day wore on and the humidity returned, but for a few hours, we had the perfect road trip weather. I looked at Milly stretched out across the backseat, smiling, her arm resting on the windowsill. The longer she was with us, the less important it seemed that she had a gun. She's one of us now, just another traveler on the road.

Rue was reading a paperback. She liked crime novels. A shocking murder, a dedicated detective, a helpless female.

Milly leaned forward and said something to Rue. They acted like old friends now.

"The last few years have been a weird, weird trip," Milly said. "Accidents, coincidences, synchronicity, and just plain old bad luck."

Rue closed her book and looked at Milly. "I have no earthly idea what you are talking about."

"You asked me how I got here. Well, I shouldn't be in this car. I should be sitting behind a desk at the University of Wisconsin. Twelve credits away from graduation."

Milly took a breath and continued. "Three years ago, I attended a meeting at the student union about ending the war. This guy, Paul, was talking about coming together to fight American imperialism. I guess that was his name; it's the one he gave me. I'd never heard anyone speak like that, the passion in his voice, the idea that students could change world events. Hearing someone say things like that out loud was what I thought students needed to hear. Adults could afford to turn their backs on the war because they weren't dying over there. The average age of a soldier killed in Vietnam is nineteen. Too young to buy beer, too young to vote, but old enough to die in a war.

"I don't think I want to hear any of this," Rue said.

"That's tough because I need to tell someone," Milly said, lighting a cigarette. "At the next meeting, Paul said he was looking for volunteers to organize a campus protest. I raised my hand. For the next two weeks, I stood in front of the student union asking people to join the protest, handing out leaflets, and talking about the war.

The more I talked, the angrier I got. We had to do something. The war had to be stopped.

"At least Paul was doing something. He was passionate about ending the war and took every opportunity to speak out about ending the killing. I thought that if I got close to him, some of his passion would rub off on me. I didn't know who else he was sleeping with, and I didn't care.

Milly tossed her cigarette out the window.

"It rained the day of the big protest, probably why so few students came. Or maybe they just didn't care. Why should they care about a war ten thousand miles away? We marched across campus, past the administration building, and up the steps at the student union. Paul stood on the top step with a bullhorn, trying to excite the crowd. A group of cops with batons stood across the street watching us. Then Paul started taunting the cops, shouting how they were part of the white power structure. Calling 'em pigs and fascists. Someone threw a rock at the cops, and then it was a shower of rocks and bottles. The cops charged across the street, swinging their sticks. Everyone ran, except Paul. He just stood there waiting for them. I grabbed his arm and tried to pull him away, but a cop hit him across the head, and he went down. I tried to run, but another cop grabbed my hair and threw me to the ground. He put his boot on my back, shouting in my face, "Fucking hippie slut."

"They took about twenty of us downtown, and we spent the night in jail. It was awesome. We sang songs and talked all night about the war. The official charge was

disturbing the peace. We paid a fine, and they released us. At the next meeting, two new faces showed up. Ricky and Greg
Armstrong. They weren't students. They were a little older, more serious, and worked in town as electricians. Their cousin had died in Vietnam, and they wanted to help. After the protest, the meetings got smaller and smaller. Paul talked less about the war and politics and more about doing something. Making a statement to show the world we were serious. Violence is the only language they understand, he'd say. I can't remember when I first heard the word bomb.

Milly sat back, pulling her fingers through her hair. "There's got to be a better way to mark the passage of time. Time should be measured by strong emotional memories, rage, regret, sadness, and desire, instead of by seconds, minutes, and years. I don't think I'll ever feel that strongly about anything again.

"It was only three years ago. Feels like yesterday. Paul was the one who came up with the plan. The university had just landed a Department of Defense contract. Our school was now part of the war effort. We need to show those fuckers we mean business, Paul said, no more lame protests, leaflets, or speeches.

"Ricky bought a hundred gallons of fuel oil at a service station, then drove to a farmers' co-op and got about twelve hundred pounds of ammonium nitrate fertilizer. The afternoon before the bomb, Paul stole an old panel van and drove it out into the country where Ricky and Greg were waiting. They assembled the bomb, set the electronic timer, and then drove to my dorm. My job was a getaway driver. I wasn't nervous. I was excited. We ordered pizza and smoked a few joints to calm down, but the weed only made us more jittery and paranoid.

"A little after three in the morning, Ricky drove to the engineering building and parked out front. All the lights were off. Paul was across campus in his room. Greg and I were a few blocks away in my car, waiting for Ricky. When he climbed into the car, Greg gave him a hug, and I drove away. We didn't go far. I drove to a Waffle House near campus, and we ordered breakfast and waited.

Milly lit another cigarette. "No one was supposed to get hurt; the building was supposed to be empty." She took a long drag and blew the smoke out the window. "It wasn't. A graduate student, married with two kids, was killed as he came out of the building. He'd gone to his office to get his notes for class. I found out the next day in the newspaper. Ricky and Greg left town immediately.

"A few hours later, Paul knocked on my door. He didn't look right. I'm gonna tell you something I probably shouldn't, he said, I'm an informant for the FBI. It felt like someone had kicked me in the stomach. He was leaving town and said I should split as well. So, I packed a bag, emptied my bank account, and bought a bus ticket for San Francisco."

7

Alabama did not offer much in the way of scenery. The highway was nearly empty. Thick pine trees grew along the edge of the road. Rusty wire fence strung between worn cedar posts. An empty tire swing hung from a tree. We passed an old man in overalls standing in his yard yelling at his dog, the animal doing happy circles across the grass.

Rue was asleep again, slumped against the door. Milly was quiet, looking out the window. I wanted to turn on the radio for some music, but didn't want to wake up Rue. I looked in the rearview mirror, and Milly caught my glance.

"What does your old man do for a living?"

"He was in the army, now he owns a feed store."

"And one day you'll inherit the business."

"Maybe…I dunno. I work there after school on some days."

"I'll bet he's a pain to work for."

"He's got a lot of rules."

"What about your mom?"

"My mom is…a happy drunk."

I surprised myself. I had never described my Mother like that before, but that's what she was. By the time I got home from school in the afternoon, she was already feeling no pain. Moving slowly around the kitchen. Always with a glass of wine in her hand. When my father got home, she'd sit quietly at the dinner table, a distracted smile on her face, listening to my father rant about stupid customers or the latest evidence that the country was going to hell.

"I'm never getting married," Milly said. "I don't see the advantage."

"Maybe you haven't met the right person yet."

"I've certainly met a lot of the wrong people."

"You don't want to be alone, do you?"

"Being a woman is like belonging to a political party that's never in power. You're always looking in from the outside."

I glanced at her in the mirror. She had a wide mouth under a thin nose. Her dark hair was parted in the middle. She was smiling, but I couldn't tell if she was serious. Everything she said sounded sarcastic.

"Keep your eyes on the road, Jimbo."

We rode in silence for a while, the sun moving higher in the sky, light streaming through the trees. There were only a few old log trucks on the road. Thankfully, we hadn't seen any cops.

In the distance, I saw what looked like a low cloud hanging just above the tree line. The road curved around a hill, and the land opened into a wide field of cotton bordered by a dense stand of trees. The trees along the edge of the field were on fire. Thick smoke billowed out across the rows of cotton. Bright flames engulfed the pine trees. A farmer stood next to his tractor, watching the fire move closer to his crop.

"Pull over," Milly shouted.

I guided the Caddy onto the shoulder of the highway. Milly climbed out of the car, jumped the fence, and ran toward the farmer. I looked at Rue; her eyes were shut, her head against the door.

A dense gray smoke hung low over the cotton field. My eyes were stinging when I caught up with Milly and the farmer. He was pointing to the burning trees at the edge of his field.

"The fire's gonna jump over into my cotton," he
shouted. "I'm gonna lose it all."

He took off his sweat-stained baseball cap, wiped his forehead, and climbed up on the tractor. He handed us burlap sacks, pointed to the flames, and started up the machine.

We followed behind the tractor through the field until we were close to the burning trees. The smoke was thicker now, billowing out over rows of cotton, the glowing trees crackling and snapping. Orange flames blossomed like flowers. The heat is too intense to get any closer. The farmer lowered the plow and began turning the dirt over, moving slowly along the edge of the fire.

Milly held the sack over her face to block the fierce heat and smoke. "He's making a firewall," she yelled, pointing to the tall grass, already on fire, at the edge of the field. Small rivers of flame were moving out of the burning trees toward the rows of cotton. She began beating the burning grass with the sack. I did the same. We worked our way slowly behind the tractor. The intense heat and smoke made it hard to keep my eyes open. My lungs were burning, but I kept slashing at the flames with the sack. It seemed hopeless. No sooner did we extinguish the small grass fires than sparks from the burning trees landed on the cotton and set it on fire. Milly ran between the rows, slapping at the flames. The smoke was thicker now; it was difficult to breathe. I couldn't see Milly or the farmer. I felt dizzy and sat down, covering my head with the burlap. Milly appeared through the thick smoke, grabbing my arms, pulling me away from the fire.

When he reached the far end of his field, the farmer shut off the tractor and climbed down. He stood there with his hands on his hips, watching the flames move closer to his crop. I staggered toward the road, coughing, trying to get away from the flames and the smoke.

Milly and the farmer stood and watched as the wind shifted, lifting the low-hanging smoke up and carrying it away from the cotton. The fire was losing intensity, and the flames were running out of fuel. The trees had burned clear down to bare trunks, leaving a forest of black, smoking poles.

Milly and the farmer worked their way along the fence line, beating out the last of the small, stubborn fires.

I put my hand to my face; it felt hot, like a bad sunburn. Every breath was a struggle, my lungs full of smoke. I looked across the field at the Caddy parked on the side of the road. Rue was leaning against the fender, watching. I waved at her. She waved back.

The farmer lived at the end of a red dirt road in an old frame house with a sagging roof. He was standing on the front porch when we pulled up. The three of us climbed out and stood in the shaded yard. The farmer's face and arms were covered with soot and ash.

"Y'all hungry?" he asked.

Rue stepped forward and said, "We don't want to inconvenience you."

"We appreciate your help. Let us return the favor."

We stepped inside the house. The farmer pointed to a long table, and we all took a seat. His wife was standing in a small kitchen, ladling beans into bowls. She carried them to the table and set them in front of us.

"Eat," she said sharply, "before it gets cold."

I looked around the small room. What little furniture they had was old and worn.

The wife pulled a large iron skillet out of the oven, placing it in the center of the table. The smell of warm cornbread filled the room. She sat down next to her husband and looked up.

"We hold hands and say grace over our meals," she said.

We all reached out, holding hands, the farmer bowing his head. "For the food we are about to receive, may the Lord make us truly thankful. Amen."

I spooned the hot beans into my mouth and looked around. My eyes were still burning from the smoke. The table was quiet. The excitement of fighting the fire had brought us together; we were tired strangers, not sure what to say to each other. No one spoke for several long minutes until Rue looked up and smiled at the wife.

"I believe these are the best beans I've ever put in my mouth."

The woman smiled. "Bacon grease. That's the secret."

I knew Rue had grown up on a farm, but didn't realize how much she knew about cotton. She asked the farmer about the amount of rainfall per year, the types of fertilizers he used, and where he processed his crop. They talked about the see-sawing price of cotton, how every year was another chance to go further into debt. The farmer sat back in his chair, relaxed now, eager to discuss the struggles of working his land.

After we finished the meal, we said our goodbyes on the porch and climbed into the Caddy. Milly is behind the wheel now. As we rolled down the dirt road toward the highway, Rue looked back at the old house, the farmer and his wife standing on the porch.

"Grandson, you could do worse than that."

8

I lay down on the backseat watching the clouds through the window, and for some reason I thought about my sister. One morning, about a year ago, I walked into the kitchen and found my Mother standing at the counter drinking coffee. "Your sister left home last night."

I asked if she'd run away or if she left with someone.

"She's gone, what does it matter?"

In my mind, there was a big difference, but it didn't seem the right time to discuss it with her. My Mother walked to the living room and sat on the sofa. She seemed quietly agitated, as though unsure how to react to her eldest child walking away from the family. Over the years, the alcohol had done something to my Mother's face, blurred all the sharpness in her features, and made her skin look dull. I could tell she didn't want to talk. She wanted to sit on the sofa, watch the day slip by, and avoid any annoying emotions.

I left for school, and all day I thought about Nancy. When I got home, my Mother was still on the sofa; a wine glass had replaced the coffee mug. We never talked about why Nancy left or where she might be. And when my dad got home, we all pretended everything was fine.

I felt bad the rest of the afternoon, stretched out on the backseat, wondering if the smoke had permanently damaged my lungs. I must have fallen asleep because when I opened my eyes, it was late afternoon and we were parked at a gas station. Milly stood at the gas pump, filling up the Caddy.

I climbed out of the car. "Where's Rue?"

"Bathroom."

"Where are we?"

"Mississippi."

The sun was behind the trees now, casting long shadows across the road.

I looked up and saw a young man, dressed in a purple suit, carrying a leather case, standing in front of the gas station. He walked over and smiled at Milly. "Good afternoon."

Milly looked at him. "Hello."

He set the case down and laced his fingers together. "I'm just off the bus coming from Detroit, and I find myself in a jam." He spoke slowly, in no rush to tell his story. "I have a job waiting for me in Bay St. Louis, and I have no money for a bus ticket. And to make things more interesting, the job begins in a few hours."

"What kind of job?" Milly said.

He gestured at the case at his feet. "A man hired me to play the horn for Jimmy Reed. Three nights, starting tonight."

"Who's Jimmy Reed?" I said.

He turned to look at me, nodding. "Yeah…makes sense you don't know who Jimmy Reed is."

"Do you need some money?" Milly said.

"Money is good. But the gig starts in four hours, and I'm about a hundred miles from the stage."

"I'd say yes if this were my car, but the lady who owns it has the final word."

Rue came out of the gas station and walked over to the Caddy. The three of us stood listening while the horn player repeated his story. Rue was quiet, both hands on her purse. It was hard to tell what she was thinking from the look on her face. She always looked suspicious, even when she smiled, which wasn't often. The horn player stopped talking, and we waited for Rue to say something. As the silence went on, I wanted to speak, to break the tension.

"The funeral is Sunday," I said, "and today is only Thursday. It's only a couple hours out of our way…"

"I know when the funeral is," Rue snapped. "I just want to know when this outing turned into a damn bus service for the penniless and the stranded. First this one…" She pointed at Milly, then gestured at the horn player. "Now this tall drink of water…and you." She slapped me on the back of my head. "All this nonsense, young man. You are straining my last frayed nerve." Rue looked up at the young man standing in front of her. "Well…I like your suit, and you don't smell bad."

9

The horn player's name was Lester Berryhill. "Most folks call me Shade," he said, explaining how the rest of his family is a shade darker than he is. So he became Shade.

"How could that happen," I said, "your family dark and you light-skinned?"

He looked at me. "Black folks weren't just for picking cotton. They were for making more field hands."

"What kind of music do you play?"

"Any kind of man wants me to play. Gospel, jazz, rock & roll, R & B. It all comes from the same tree." "What tree?" I said.

He looked at me, unsure how to answer. "The tree of slavery. Without slavery, music in this country would be nothing but Pat Boone, Bing Crosby, and Doris Day."

He closed his eyes, but I wouldn't leave him alone. I wanted to talk.

"Where are you from?"

"You don't smoke, do you, boy?"

I shook my head.

Shade leaned forward and spoke to Rue. "I wonder if I might trouble you for a cigarette, ma'am?" Rue handed him a cigarette and a lighter. He lit the cigarette and smoked in silence, looking out the window for a long while, then said, "I was born not too far from here, a place called Pistol Ridge. Not even a town, really, just a church and a gas station. My Daddy was in the lumber trade and owned his own flatbed truck. Used to haul logs up to Hattiesburg. Made a decent living."

He was quiet again, smoking.

"Then what happened?"

He laughed. "Mississippi happened, rednecks happened."

I couldn't tell if he was disgusted or amused.

He pointed at me with the cigarette. "How old are you, boy?"

"Eighteen."

He nodded. "Old enough to ask the question, dumb enough to not understand the answer."

Was he mocking me now? I thought.

"Medgar Evers, Dr. King, Malcolm X. Know who those people are?"

"I know who Dr. King is. Was."

"Good for you." He turned to look out the window.

"Why did you leave Mississippi?"

Rue turned in her seat, waiting for him to answer.

Shade took a drag on the cigarette, letting the smoke drift from his mouth.

"My Daddy was a deacon of his church. He took on the task of organizing voter registration in the county. Every Sunday, after service, he'd stand in the doorway telling folks this was the year. 1964. Black folk are gonna make their voices heard. The federal government passed a law, and we can vote now. No poll tax, no literacy test, no crackers standing in our way.

"A lot of white people didn't like what he was up to, some of 'em said it to his face. Telling him the black man ain't ready for the vote, not in this state. The phone would ring late at night, I'd pick it up, and there would be nobody on the other end. Cars are driving by the house, lights off. Dead animals left on the porch. Paint was thrown on his truck.

"One night, the phone rang, and it was the white man Daddy worked with. Known this fella for years. He says, Deacon, you've got two hours to get out of the county. Two hours. My old man was too stubborn to listen. Woe unto them that call good evil, he says, and evil good.

Shade rolled down the window and flipped the cigarette out.

"I don't believe in good or evil. It's just folks wanting things real bad, then doing whatever it takes to get them. The deacon said we are staying. Loads his shotgun and sits by the front door. Mother tells him it's not worth it, let's pack up and leave. We'll come back when all this is over. When will that be, the deacon says, " A couple of hundred years?

"Some folks think hate can be overcome by knowledge. They wrong. Hate is older than knowledge, old as rocks and water. It's in here." He tapped his chest. "Not up here." He pointed to my head.

It was quiet in the car; we were all listening.

"Know why bad people always come looking for you in the middle of the night?" Shade said. "'Cause they're afraid to let folks see their faces. They cowards. They shot the deacon when he opened the front door and leveled that shotgun at 'em. Tossed firebombs through the front window and up on the roof. We ran out the back, down the road to a neighbor's house. Sat in that lady's kitchen and watched our house burn. It was gone in minutes.

"The deacon didn't die right away. He lay up in the hospital a few days before he gave it up."

A hardness came over Shade's face. He turned to look out the window.

I knew not to ask any more questions.

The car was quiet for miles.

After a while, Shade leaned forward and spoke to Milly and Rue. "I believe I could use a drink. Would you ladies care to join me? Gotta be five o'clock somewhere."

10

I stayed in the car while they went into the liquor store. The sun was almost down now, and cars had their headlights on. Through the store window, I could see Milly and Shade talking, moving slowly down the aisles. Rue stood at the counter, waiting. She knew what she wanted. Scotch was her drink, two fingers in a short glass, no ice, no water. Sometimes in the summer, when it was hot and humid, she might add an ice cube. Then she'd sit on her screened porch and watch the birds in her yard. She kept a loaded pellet gun by the back door for the neighborhood cats. Rue hated cats because they killed birds. When she saw a cat slinking through her yard, she'd grab the rifle, slowly open the back door, and let the animal have it. Her eyesight wasn't that great, so she rarely hit her target. The neighbors had warned her for years that if she killed one of their cats, they'd call the cops on her. Go ahead, Rue would say, I'd love to see 'em arrest an old lady.

They all came back to the car, smiling. Rue had a pint of Johnny Walker Black. Milly had a six-pack of Cokes and a bottle of Bacardi rum. She pointed at me, "You're driving, sport." Shade took two Cokes, poured half of each in the dirt, opened the rum, and filled the cans. Rue sat in the front seat, the open bottle of Scotch on her lap. She lifted it and said, "Chinchin!" And took a long drink.

"What's that mean?" I said.

"It means, yes, please."

"Let's go, boy," Shade said. "We're burning daylight."

I eased the Caddy out onto the highway and, in no time, they were all smiling, laughing. I could see why people love to drink. Who doesn't want to be instantly happy?

Milly leaned forward and asked Rue how long she'd been married.

"The first time? Or the second time?"

"Wait," I said, "you were married before?"

She looked at me. "Yes, I was. Man's name was John Earl Chapman. I took his name, and when he passed, I dropped it. Our marriage started out with a misunderstanding and never recovered."

The car went quiet. Rue took a sip from the pint. "That marriage was about learning to love people I didn't really like. Didn't like his Mother or his sister, and I didn't like it when he dragged me back to Texas. The only good thing to come out of that marriage was that he taught me how to drive. Growing up, I'd watch my father and Percy work the gears and dials on our truck. I'd never been the least bit curious, never anticipated that one day I'd be sitting behind the wheel. Driving a car was just one of those skills I never considered learning.

"One morning, John drove me to the middle of a pasture near our home, braked to a stop, and got out. I climbed into the driver's seat, put my hands on the wheel, and looked out the window. He began to lecture me about the internal combustion engine and how it transferred power from the pistons to the drive train and then to the wheels. To be honest, I wasn't listening. I was imagining the places I wanted to go, the roads I would soon be rolling down, the new folks I would meet. I felt like a cage was opening and I was being set free.

"When he stopped talking, I looked at him and said, Let's give it a try. He told me to press the clutch to the floor and engage the gears. The machine made a loud, grinding metallic noise, then I felt the gears slide into place. I lifted my foot, and the car jumped forward and stalled. We repeated this two-footed maneuver several times, all with the same outcome, until at last I was able to finesse the machine into motion. The car began to move slowly over the grass while I sat calmly behind the wheel, guiding the machine. It felt wonderful. John ran alongside the car, shouting at me. I pushed the accelerator and the car shot forward. He began to run faster. Shift to second, he shouted.

"I pressed the clutch down, pulled back the stick, and lifted my foot. Now the car was moving briskly across the pasture. I looked up and saw two cowboys sitting on their horses at the far edge of the field, watching my progress. I lifted my hand and waved at them. The men touched the brims of their hats.

"I pressed the clutch to the floor and shifted into the next gear, and the car motored forward. I turned the wheel, and the car quickly climbed a low hill. In the distance, I could see the trees that grew along the edge of the creek, the hills beyond the trees, and the blue sky above. What I didn't see was the barbed-wire fence. The wire snagged the front bumper, and the momentum of the automobile pulled up fence posts until the vehicle came to a stop. The wire snapped and flew back toward the car in a snarling mass of cedar posts and barbed wire. The wire was so tightly wound around the car that I couldn't open either door. Had to wait until John ran back to the house for a pair of fence cutters.

"By the time he returned, the two cowboys had ridden over to see if they could help. They sat on their horses, watching John cut the wire, pulling it free. All four tires were punctured, and there were deep scratches in the paint. Finally, one of the cowboys spoke. She's a good little driver, he said, but she's awfully hard on the equipment."

11

On one of those rare days when I was paying attention in science class, the teacher said something that stayed with me. Our body's cells are dying and being replicated all the time, she said, and in seven years every cell in your body will be replaced. We are a new person every seven years. Here I was, over halfway through the third iteration of James Birdwell, wondering how many versions of myself I had to look forward to.

An hour down the road, all the drinkers needed a restroom. It was dark now, and we were still about fifty miles from Bay St. Louis. I rolled into a gas station, and everyone climbed out. The bottle of Scotch was nearly empty, the gas gauge half full. The Caddy was a gas hog, but we might be able to make it without another stop. Hungry and tired, I climbed out of the car and stretched.

A car pulled off the highway and came to a stop at the gas pumps. I read the words on the door: Stone County Sheriff Department. Shade and Milly came around the side of the building just as the cop stepped out of his car. Shade had his arm around Milly's shoulder. The cop turned to watch them stroll back to the car. It was still rare in the South to see a black man with a white woman. Was that what he was looking at? Or had he heard about the robbery? My heart beat a little faster.

We've been seen, I thought, now we were being looked over.

I was the only one sober enough to drive, but I didn't look old enough. With everyone back in the car, I pulled slowly out onto the highway. In the mirror, I could see the cop standing with his door open, talking on his radio.

A few miles down the road, headlights came up fast behind us. We were being followed. I looked at the speedometer, well under the speed limit. Everyone was still happy; no one but me had noticed the cop.

"I think we're being followed," I said.

They all turned to look out the back window.

Flashing red lights and a siren. I let the Caddy roll off the road onto the shoulder. Everyone was quiet now. My window was already down when the cop walked up. I handed him my license. He didn't say anything, just leaned over and looked inside. "Who's your friend in the back?"

"Just a…person who we know. We're giving him a ride."

"Looks like a pimp."

"He's a musician," I said. "He has a job in Bay St. Louis."

"That right, boy? Are you a musician?"

Shade didn't answer. He looked straight ahead.

"Is there a problem, officer?" Milly said.

"Have you been drinking, miss?"

"That's none of your business."

The cop laughed. "This badge says it's my fucking business. A black man with a white woman being chauffeured by a kid with grandma riding shotgun. Something ain't right here."

He made all of us climb out of the Caddy while he searched the car. When he didn't find anything, he looked upset and took everyone's driver's license except Milly's.

"Where's your license?" the cop said.

"I lost my purse, had all my stuff in it," Milly said.

"What's your name?"

She paused, then said, "Stacy O'Neil. I'm on my way to a funeral with Jim and Rue."

The cop stared at Milly. "I don't believe a word coming out of your mouth."

The cop walked to his car and climbed inside. We could see him on the radio, checking the licenses.

Milly looked at Shade. "You got any overdue tickets…outstanding warrants?"

"Not in this state, but Mississippi doesn't need a reason to haul you to jail."

After what seemed like an hour, the cop walked slowly back to the Caddy and handed us back our licenses. He stepped close to Shade. "I want you to put your hands on the hood…now."

"What for, man?"

The cop grabbed Shade's arm and pushed him toward the car.

"This ain't right," Shade said. "You got no cause."

"Shut the fuck up."

Shade put his hands on the hood.

"You got anything on you, boy?"

"I always carry a pocketknife," Shade said.

"Pull it out," the cop said, "show it to me."

The cop stepped back and put a hand on his pistol.

"No, sir. Not gonna do that. The knife is in my back pocket if you want to see it."

"I told you to show me your knife," the cop shouted.

No one moved. The night was quiet, the highway empty. Somewhere back in the shadows, crickets were making noise. The cop shouted again for Shade to show him the knife. Shade shook his head. "Not gonna do it."

Rue stepped forward and put her hand on Shade's shoulder.

"Officer, I'm going to reach into this young man's pocket and show you the knife...ok?"

The cop was quiet, one hand on his pistol. He looked frozen, not sure what to do.

"Did you hear me?" Rue said. After a long pause, the cop nodded. Rue reached into Shade's pocket and pulled out the knife. The cop grabbed it, threw it into the bushes, turned, and walked back to his car. I waited until the cop car accelerated down the highway and then eased out onto the road. Everyone was laughing now, calling the cop names. Shade rolled down his window and lifted his middle finger into the night air.

12

I know more about my next-door neighbors than I do about Robert Charles Birdwell, my old man. Rue told me once she regretted sending him away to military school when he was twelve. The experience made him very quiet, she said. After graduation, he joined the army and spent most of the Korean War in California as a procurement officer. Instead of being sent to the fight, he learned the business of buying and selling, supply chains, and inventory. He hated it, but that's what the army ordered him to do. So that's what he did. My father is a man with a strong faith in rules and order. SOP, he calls it. Standard Operating Procedure. He learned that in the army and was never able to unlearn it in civilian life. According to Rue's version of events, he met my Mother in California at the beach while on leave.

I can imagine that. Robert Birdwell is an impressive looking man. Well over six feet tall, with wide shoulders and a prominent nose, sitting in the middle of a calm face. Perhaps my Mother mistook his subdued personality for a deep intelligence. And he is an intelligent man. He reads and understands the issues, but his views on the world were formed decades ago, and he is resolutely determined never to change his opinions. Inconsistency might be mistaken for a character flaw. According to my father, the world is a battleground, good versus evil, communism versus capitalism.

If you are against the Vietnam War, you are against everything he believes in, and two hundred young Americans shipped home in body bags every week won't change his opinion. It's just the price we pay for living in the greatest country on earth.

I was still behind the wheel, heading south now. The Caddy's headlights lit up a small patch of dark, empty highway. The clock on the dashboard read a little after seven. Rue was asleep, her bottle empty on the seat. Milly and Shade were sitting close, talking, his arm around her shoulder.

"Turn on the radio, Jimbo," Milly said.

I switched it on, turning the dial, looking for some good tunes. All I found were livestock reports, screaming preachers, and country music.

"Shut it off," Shade said, "hurtin' my ears."

I glanced in the mirror, and Shade caught my eye. "What are you looking at, boy?"

He sounded angry and maybe a little drunk.

"When you left Mississippi," I said, "where did you go?" "Just shut your mouth and drive, kid," Milly said.

"No, no…boy wants to know. How is he gonna know

less if he asks questions?"

He leaned forward. "I got a question for you, boy. Who freed more minds, Abraham Lincoln or Jimi Hendrix?"

I started to say something, and he interrupted me. "Doesn't require an answer, son. Just something to think about."

I didn't care if he was pissed off; I wanted to know more. "Where did you go after Mississippi?"

Shade paused, then said, "We jumped out of the frying pan into the fire. Left Pistol Ridge directly after the funeral and drove north to Detroit, stayed with my aunt. I was about your age, didn't know shit. Just the three of us. My Mother, my older brother Luther, and I. None of us liked Detroit, too cold. Luther started to get into all kinds of trouble. Got thrown out of school, spent some time in jail. A few years later, during the riot, man finally found his calling. What saved me was that horn in the trunk. My uncle played jazz on the weekends, showed me the basics, and I took it from there. Luther didn't have a horn; all he had was an almighty hatred for white folks."

"What riot?"

"The Detroit Riot, four days of looting, shooting, and disputing. Luther loved that shit. Every night, he and his boys out there shooting up the streets."

"How long did it last?"

"Four, five days. They called in the Guard. Tanks rolling down Claremont, soldiers on every street corner. That settled everybody down."

"What happened to Luther?"

"Joined the army, got trained up, and sent to Vietnam. Man gave him a gun, told him he could shoot anybody he
wanted."

13

Three moves are as good as a housefire, my Mother used to say. And we moved a lot. A few photo albums are all the evidence we ever lived in any of those army towns. My Mother only accumulated the bare minimum. No furniture handed down from family, no knick-knacks, no souvenirs, or mementos. The inside of all our houses looked as plain as a hotel room. All our furniture and personal stuff had to fit on one small moving truck. With very few reminders of my past, I looked at everything in my life as temporary, transitional. Houses, family, friends, schools. My life could be uprooted at a moment's notice, and nothing I did made any difference. Sounds like a curse you might wish on your enemies. But once you accept the idea of no permanent address and everything constantly changing, the disruptions become a license to do as you please.

I pulled up in front of an old wooden house with cars parked carelessly across the lawn. A large tour bus stood at the curb. A constant stream of people moved in and out of the front door. The small house pulsated with music. Over the door was a sign: 100 Men Hall.

Shade climbed out of the car and lifted his case out of the trunk. He leaned in the window. "You all are welcome to come inside as my guests. Not you, boy, not of age. You might see things that could corrupt your young mind." He smiled at me and walked into the house.

We found a place for the night across the street from the ocean, a few run-down tourist cabins with a crushed oyster shell driveway. Palm trees and Spanish oaks shaded the seedy cabins. It was dark, and we hadn't eaten all day. We bought some hamburgers and ate them while looking out over the smooth ocean. The night sky was clear, and a few stars began to appear. Low waves rolled in under the pier, making whispering sounds.

Hours later, I sat in a chair in the cabin waiting for Rue. She was in the bathroom, where she'd been for almost an hour. I'd seen Milly smoking a cigarette outside earlier; now the lights were off in her cabin. I knew where she'd gone. The same place I was headed once the old lady was asleep.

When I stepped out of the cabin, I heard the sounds in the distance, a pounding pulse like an excited heartbeat. I locked the door and walked toward the music.

There was a large man standing at the door of the 100 Men Hall when I stepped up on the porch. He folded his arms, rolling a toothpick from one side of his mouth to the other.

"Don't even ask," he said.

I offered him a fifty, money I'd taken from Rue's purse. He shook his head and laughed.

"How's fifty bucks gonna help me when I lose my liquor license, boy?"

Standing there on the porch, I felt the boards under my feet vibrating. The house shook. Music blasted from every window, pouring out through the walls, through the roof. Every time the door swung open, the volume increased, and I could see the sweaty crowd moving up and down. Dancers dripping wet, the smell of sweat, beer, and liquor. The house seemed to be drawing everyone toward the pounding music. I stood on the porch waiting for the door to swing open so I could see inside. When I refused to leave, the bouncer pushed me off the porch onto the lawn. I'd never heard music like that before. Deep, pulsing, hypnotic. I stood on the lawn, unable to leave, the rhythmic beat moving up from my feet through my body. I could feel every note deep in my chest. The bouncer tried to chase me away, but I kept coming back, standing on the lawn so I could see inside when the door opened. Finally, he gave up and let me stay.

Later that night, the band took a break. They stood on the lawn under the stars, smoking cigarettes. Seven identical purple suits over white ruffled shirts. Jimmy Reed and The Chicago All Stars. Shade looked over and lifted his cigarette to acknowledge me.

My legs felt like rubber, and I had to piss. I walked around behind the house to find a place to do my business. As I came around the corner, I saw a woman leaning back on the hood of a car, her dress up over her hips. A man stood in front of her, unbuckling his belt. She looked up at me and said, "Run along, child."

The band played deep into the night. Then the music stopped abruptly, and the lawn was suddenly crowded with sweaty bodies, women fanning themselves with their hands, men lighting cigarettes. I sat on the porch, watching the crowd drift off into the clear night. I looked around for Milly but couldn't find her, so I walked back to the cabin. My heart pounding, my head scrambled with these new sounds.

A light was on in Milly's cabin. I stood at her door and heard voices. Maybe she was awake. I had to tell somebody about how this music made me feel; this couldn't wait until morning. I started to knock and stopped when I heard laughing inside. It was Shade. I stood at her door for a long time, trying to think of what to do, trying not to do something stupid and embarrass myself.

After a while, I walked around to the back of her cabin. A window was open, and a light was on. I found a cinder block, put it under the window, and looked in. The bathroom door was open, and Milly was standing in front of the bed, swaying back and forth in her underwear. She was holding her camera. Shade's purple suit was draped over a chair. He was laughing, saying something to her. She stepped to the front door, locked it, and lay across the bed. White legs and black legs laced together. The things I was seeing in that room merged with the blues hammering in my head. I couldn't name what I was feeling, but I liked it.

14

When I woke the next morning, Rue was standing in the open door, smoking a cigarette. She had already loaded our suitcases in the trunk.

"I'm driving today," she said.

She handed me a ten-dollar bill and told me to go find breakfast.

In the daylight, Bay St. Louis looked a lot different. The houses were older, a little rundown, and most needed a coat of paint. There were no sidewalks or curbs, but lots of potholes. I wandered down the street looking for a corner store, still feeling good from the night before. The sky was unreal, a vivid, intense blue you rarely see if you don't live near the coast. The last few stars were fading into a bright sky. The air was cool, the ocean a few blocks away. I could smell it. It was still early, no cars on the street, a few people walking to work. A kid on a bike rode toward me. I lifted my hand. "Hey, do you know where there's a store around here?" He shook his head and kept pedaling.

Down another street and past a warehouse, I found a small grocery store and bought four honey buns, a six-pack of Coke, and a newspaper. The headline stretched across the front page, in tall, bold letters: Space Men Fight for Life. And underneath the headline: Astronauts struggle to make it back to Earth. There was a picture of the capsule. They were stranded hundreds of thousands of miles from Earth in a metal can not much bigger than a Cadillac. Out their window, the astronauts could see their blue home hanging in the cold blackness. What were their chances of making it back alive?

Milly and Rue were sitting in the front seat of the Caddy when I got back to the cabins.

"Where's Shade?" I said.

"Still asleep," Milly said.

"I want to tell him goodbye."

"Leave him be. He didn't get much sleep."

Wonder why, I thought.

Rue climbed into the Caddy and started the engine. Milly stretched out across the backseat and closed her eyes. I slid in next to Rue and, in minutes, we were cruising down the interstate and soon out of Mississippi. The highway crossed several creeks that ran deep into the green landscape. Wide oak trees with Spanish moss hanging from the branches. Still, black water in the quiet swamps crowding the highway. The heat and humidity were back. Dense, bulky clouds flowed across the blue sky, like boxcars on a train.

With her hair pulled back, smiling, Rue looked different that morning. If I wanted to know more about her, I'd better ask while she was in a good mood.

"Tell me about your first husband?"

Rue sighed. "John Earl Chapman. A very pleasant man to look at, he had a nice smile. Tall, wide shoulders, nice hair. I was young, and he was handsome, that's about all I'm gonna say about that."

"Where did you meet him?"

She smiled. "You writing a book, Jim?"

"No ma'am. I just want to know more about my family."

Rue reached out and took my hand. "When I was your age, I had very few things but lots of time. Now I've got everything I want and very little time."

It was hard to imagine Rue as a young woman, someone with doubts and fears. She always seemed to know exactly what she wanted and always had an opinion about everything. If she ever had a moment of uncertainty, she rarely showed it.

"I won't talk about John Earl, but I'll tell you how I came to live in Oklahoma. One Sunday, our pastor introduced us to Milton Wilder, superintendent of the Oklahoma School for the Deaf. He didn't look much older than me, but when he stepped forward and spoke passionately about his school's need for people who would be willing to help others in need, his message touched me. Up until then, I'd been living a routine life. Suddenly, another path opened for me, a new future. My heart had been transformed…a spiritual awakening, I suppose. A few weeks later, I was in Oklahoma, ready to begin a new life.

"My job was to bring deaf children to our school. Milton warned me it would not be easy. Parents of deaf children were very protective and reluctant to let them go. To parents, a deaf child is a special soul in need of God's extra care. There is a strong bond between a Mother and her deaf child, he said, a bond that will come between you and your task."

Rue paused, and for a second her eyes darkened. "On a cool morning in late September, I put my bag on the back seat of the Ford and climbed behind the wheel. I remember the sky that morning. A vivid, unbroken sky stretched from horizon to horizon, as if a blue dome of air had been lowered over the land. Not a single cloud. Oklahoma had few paved roads in 1918 and even fewer motor cars. In my entire life, I don't believe I've had a more enjoyable journey than I did that morning. Sitting behind the wheel, the warm sun on my face.

"Who among us, when embarking on a new undertaking, can possibly anticipate all the stumbles and missteps waiting in our path? It was dusk when I rolled to a stop in front of the Browning house. House is a charitable description. The structure was little more than a shed, a rough wooden shelter with a single window and a door fashioned from whatever material was at hand.

"A thin dog greeted me when I stepped out of the car. I waited in the yard for a sign of life and, when no one appeared, I knocked on the door. After several minutes, a woman stepped out of the house.

"I introduced myself as an employee of the Oklahoma School for the Deaf and said I had come to escort her son to the school. The woman grabbed my arm and pulled me aside.

"My boy doesn't know," she whispered, "and neither does my husband."

"She didn't look much older than I, yet there were deep lines around her eyes."

"I will talk to your son," I said. "He will see the wisdom of your decision."

"It's not the boy," she said quickly. "It's Fred."

"Inside, her husband and son were seated at a rough table for their meal. Fred stood up when I entered the house. The boy looked at me and smiled. I introduced myself, shaking the father's hand, then the boy's. Mrs. Browning went to the kitchen, ladled soup into a bowl, and returned to the table. The father and the boy were quiet.

"This is the teacher I was telling you about," Mrs. Browning said. "She's going to take Jack to school. We can do no more for him."

"Her husband stood up from the table and stepped back. Seeing his father's reaction, the boy reached out and touched his Mother, deep worry on his young face.

"I need him here," the father said. "I can't run this place without him."

"The boy began to moan, rocking side to side slowly."

"What about Jack?" the Mother said. "Would you leave him to suffer through a life of silence, cut off from the world?"

"No school can restore his hearing," the father said.

"I asked Mr. Browning to please sit down so that we could talk. Reluctantly, he sat down. The boy went to his father and hugged him tight.

"He needs a special school with other children just like him," she begged. "We are Jack's handicap now; we are holding him back."

"After our meal, the boy went to bed. All night, I heard husband and wife whispering sharply to each other in the bedroom. I lay on a pallet in the kitchen, my mind churning in the darkness with worry and guilt. The only person who found rest that night was the boy. He lay asleep by the stove on a small cot.

"Next morning, the four of us stood in the dirt yard in front of the house. Mrs. Browning handed me a burlap sack containing Jack's few possessions and extra clothes. The boy's face was gray and blank, his eyes moving quickly from his Mother's face to his father's face.

"Mrs. Browning held her hands in front of her, then opened them to indicate a book and pointed to me. I made the same actions with my hands. The boy ran to his Mother and hugged her tight. No words could be voiced that would reflect her pain, and none could be heard by the boy to ease the parting. Then she released the boy, and I led him to the car. All this time, the father had been standing back, watching the farewell unfold. Now he came forward and held my hands to his face, tears flowing down his cheeks.

"He is all we have," he said. "Promise me you will keep him safe and care for him." Rue was quiet.

"What happened to Jack?" I said.

"Jack was very bright, one of our best students. He was with us until he turned eighteen, then he returned home."

Rue looked at me, her mouth tight. "A few years later, I drove up to a cabin where a young girl sat in the shade of a tree. She wore a dog's collar around her neck and was held to the tree by a length of chain. Nearby was an empty bowl. She was barefoot, perhaps no more than seven years old. Her face and hair were smeared with dirt. After a short conversation with her parents, I realized they had no more concern for her well-being than they would for a cow or a goat. And if it meant they were no longer responsible for their daughter's care, they were happy to have her enrolled in our school."

"That's terrible."

"We have no choice in the kind of family we are born into, boy. Or where in this wide world we are placed. But I am certain it is better to know who has your best interests at heart and who would chain you to a tree."

15

We were living in Junction City, Kansas, a few years ago. A lot of churches in that small town, churches and grain elevators. It was winter, early January. I'd gotten a new bike for Christmas, a red Schwinn Deluxe Stingray with a banana seat and raised handlebars. I didn't care how cold it was. I was out the door and on my bike. I pedaled into town, bought a cherry Slurpee and a bag of sunflower seeds, and sat outside the 7-11. This kid rides up on a bike just like mine. We stared at each other and realized we were about the same age. His name was Vernon. His dad was also in the army. In the short time I knew him, he never came over to my house, and I never went to his. I never met his parents, and he never met mine. But we were friends. We did stuff together.

Vernon had lived in Junction City longer than I had, so he knew more about the town. He knew when the trains rolled through, stopping at the farmer's co-op to load up with grain. We'd ride our bikes over to the co-op and put stacks of pennies on the track. When the train pulled out, we'd find the flattened coins in the gravel. In summer, delivery trucks left boxes of watermelons outside the grocery store in the early morning. Vernon would snag one, balancing it on his shoulder, and we'd ride over to the park, smash it open, and eat until we were stuffed.

Vernon had a paper route. Every morning, he was up early, riding through the streets, throwing papers onto front porches. Sometimes on weekends when the paper was thick with extra advertising, I'd tie a canvas bag to my bike and ride along with him. Vernon had a small transistor radio he'd bought with his paper route money. He'd tie the radio to his handlebars and cruise down the street with the volume up as loud as it would go. I don't remember what we talked about. We didn't talk much at all. The life of an army brat had made us both quiet, always watching from the outside. We both had the same bike. We liked doing the same things. That was enough.

There was a steep road close to my house with tall hedges on both sides. We called it Chicken Hill. At the bottom of the hill was a stop sign where the road intersected with a rural highway. Most of the traffic on the highway was farm trucks pulling loads of hay or cars going to the army base. We used to sit on our bikes at the top of the hill and wait until the highway was empty, then take off pedaling as fast as we could go. At the last second, we'd kick back on the brakes and slide to a stop. The one who came closest to the highway was the winner. The other one was Chicken of the Day.

Vernon usually won. He was fearless. Pedaling like a maniac, then cranking back on the brakes, putting his foot down as the bike slid sideways toward the highway. Racing flat out, side by side, down the hill, a wall of hedges blocking the traffic noise, the smooth pavement under our tires. I always lost my nerve halfway down the hill, wondering if I could bring the bike to a stop in time, easing up on the pedaling, the stop sign getting larger. Sometimes Vernon would let go of the handlebars, raise his hands over his head, and guide the bike with his knees. Then at the last second, he'd go into a sliding stop a few feet before the highway.

One morning, Vernon pedaled over to my house and knocked on my window. It was Memorial Day, a big shopping day. The newspaper was huge, with lots of advertising inserts. We loaded up the papers and rode through wet streets, singing at the tops of our lungs. When we finished delivering the papers, we rode over to Chicken Hill. It was still early, and only a few cars were on the highway. We waited until the road was clear, threw down the canvas bags, lined up our bikes, and took off. We were flying, side by side, cool air in our faces.

Our wheels were dead even, so close I could have reached out and touched him. He turned, smiled at me, and lifted his middle finger. The stop sign was getting closer. At this point, I usually bailed out, but not that day. I was determined to beat him. Only feet from the highway now. Vernon hated to lose. If he saw me gaining an inch on him, he'd lean forward and pedal faster. I cranked back on the brakes and went into a slide. But the pavement was wet, and I kept going. Vernon was a few feet ahead of me. He shot past the stop sign and onto the highway. I saw the truck just as Vernon and his bike disappeared under its wheels. The sound of the truck tires screaming to a stop seemed to go on forever. The driver jumped out, saw me, and yelled something. I turned and pushed my bike up the hill as fast as I could go.

A few days later, everyone at school was talking about the accident. Someone asked if I was going to the funeral. I shook my head. I barely knew him, I said.

Rue drove for a few hours that morning and then said she wanted to lie down in the backseat. Milly got behind the wheel while I helped Rue get settled. She leaned against the door, using her coat for a pillow, and fell asleep.

Rue is tall, like my father, with wide shoulders. That morning, she looked small in the backseat, her hands clenched together. She and my father both have an intimidating presence. When either one enters a room, the space suddenly feels occupied. The energy changes from peaceful to poised for action. Something is going to happen, you can feel it. With my father, it's usually a long speech about my weak grades or the chores I'm neglecting. With Rue, it's often advice about my future. Join the army, she'll say, not understanding the implications of joining the army while there's a war going on. Or maybe she's fully aware of what my enlisting would mean. The implication is that I need to toughen up. One of her favorite expressions is straighten up and fly right. I've never been sure what that means. Other times she'll reach for her purse, hand me five dollars, and tell me to get a haircut. I always take the money, but I rarely get a haircut.

"Just a heads up," Milly said. "I'm getting low on cash. I may need to make another withdrawal pretty soon."

"Did you spend all your money last night?" I said.

"That's what it's for. All you can do is spend it."

"You could save it, put it in a

bank." "A bank?" Milly shook her

head.

"Or you could invest it. If you don't spend it, money grows."

"Where did you hear that? Your old

man?" I nodded.

"Well, he's wrong. A bank is the worst place for cash. It's like a money graveyard. Cash is like air or water; it needs to stay in motion and travel from one hand to the next. The blessings of money are bestowed on those who are the least selfish with its distribution. Cheap, stingy people…these are not happy human beings."

She pushed her hair behind her ear. An image of her and Shade in bed floated into my head. My heart started pounding.

"Keep your eyes open," she said. "I'm looking for a small grocery or liquor store."

"I want to hold the gun this time."

She smiled at me. "Look at you, Jimbo, growing a set of balls."

She took the exit outside Lafayette and drove north, the road winding through open farmland and pine forests. We passed through a few small towns with a single gas station and a church.

"Too small," she said, "we need at least a couple thousand citizens to make this worth it."

I was getting anxious. The first robbery had taken me by surprise. There'd been no time to think about it. Now I was imagining everything that might go wrong. This was the South. People are suspicious of outsiders, and everyone is armed.

We passed a sign: Church Point City Limits. Pop. 3697. Set back from the road, we noticed a small store: Charlie's Kountry Korner.

"You gotta love the South," Milly said, pointing to the rundown store. "Only three words in their name, and two are misspelled. It's perfect."

She made a U-turn, parked the Caddy in front of the store, and reached under the seat for the pistol. "I want you to stand by the door, make sure no one wanders in."

We stepped inside. An older man sat behind the counter in a lawn chair. A large dog was asleep on the floor. Milly reached down to pet the dog. The animal didn't move. Then she pulled the gun from her jeans, showing it to the old man. The dog went crazy, up on its feet, barking, the hair on its back standing straight up. Milly told the old man to put all the money in a bag.

"Can't hear you," he said, pointing to the barking dog.

"Tell your dog to shut up," she yelled.

"Ain't my dog," the man shouted. "He just came in here to sleep."

The dog moved closer to Milly, showing its teeth, a deep, menacing growl. She pointed the gun at the dog. "Give me all the money, or I shoot the fucking dog."

"Won't bother me none, you shoot him. Don't like him, no way. Come in here, sleeps on the floor, smelling bad."

"This is a robbery, sir," I said. "Please, just give us the money, and we'll leave."

The old guy seemed to move in slow motion. He turned lazily to the cash register, adjusting his glasses on his nose, searching for the right button. The cash drawer slid open, and he carefully lifted out the bills and stuffed them in a paper bag. The dog was drooling now, its body tense. The growls had stopped. I took the bag and stepped toward the door.

"Let's go," I said to Milly.

She backed away from the dog, the gun pointed at the angry animal. "When they stop making noise, that's when they start biting."

The old man smiled. "Why don't you all take him with you? Seems to like you."

We got three hundred and twelve dollars. Not great, but not bad. Rue woke up when we got back in the car, asking why we had stopped. Cigarettes, I said. She shook her head and went back to sleep. I couldn't believe what

I was doing. Robbing people. An accomplice to a wanted fugitive. But I couldn't help myself. Whatever Milly suggested, I was all in.

I drove south, back to the interstate. Near the on-ramp, we saw a young guy with a backpack, his thumb out.

"Want to give him a ride?" I said.

She shook her head. "Too dangerous these days. And I don't want to hear anyone's life story right now."

"Have you done a lot of hitchhiking?"

"Yeah. Until it got weird, then I quit. I once made it all the way from Boston to San Francisco in three rides. First ride was with this vinyl siding salesman. Took me all the way to Nashville. Number two was a black guy just out of the army. He wanted to see the West Coast. We never touched an interstate once. It was all secondary roads and state highways. Man, he was a cautious driver. I don't think we ever went over fifty miles an hour. In Kansas, he started to lose his desire to see California. He said the vast distances out West did something strange to his head. He felt like he might disappear, and no one would notice.

"We got to talking, and he told me he'd never been with a white girl before. I said I'd never slept with a black man, so we pulled off the road and ended two droughts in one go. He dropped me off outside Denver, turned around, and headed home, saying this country was too big to see all at once. I slept that night in a field next to the interstate. Trucks struggling up the on-ramp kept me

awake all night. In the morning, I walked out of the wet grass, and the first car that came by stopped. It was a guy about my age behind the wheel. He looked me over for the longest time, trying to decide if I was a good idea or not. Took me all the way to
San Francisco.

"I've never hitchhiked before."

"Thumbing is easy if you follow a few rules. Be on your best behavior. Pitch in for gas if you can. And most importantly, avoid telling your life story. You may think it's fascinating, but to a driver alone in a car with a stranger, anything you say can and will be taken the wrong way. Remember, you are a random particle adrift in a large, strange country. You already have several strikes against you. Americans have big hearts and are willing to help someone in need, but deep down, they don't trust anyone who can't even afford bus fare.

"My worst ride was outside Rexburg, Idaho. I was trying to get to Bozeman before nightfall. It was late October, and I did not want to sleep in a cold potato field or under a picnic table. A car stopped. A girl was driving, and there was a guy asleep in the front seat. I climbed in the back and thanked her for the ride. I was a highway veteran by this time. I thought I'd seen it all.

"After a while, the guy in the front seat wakes up, sees me, and starts bitching at the girl about picking up hitchhikers. She tells him it's her car and she'll do what she wants. I'm quiet, looking out the window. The guy is getting really worked up now, waving his arms around, shouting at her. I'm trying to stay cool, but this guy is agitated, and it's making me nervous. I offer to get out of the car, but the girl shakes her head, tells him she makes her own decisions about who rides in her car, and if he doesn't shut up, she'll throw him out. And then the guy pulls a knife and starts waving it around, putting it close to her neck, telling her to shut her fucking mouth and pull over. The girl lets the car drift slowly to a stop at the edge of the road.

"We're in the middle of nowhere, trees crowding the road. It's dark. She shuts off the engine and looks at him. He's pointing the knife at her chest, telling me to get out of the car. I don't want any trouble, I said, I'm leaving. I open the door to step out, and the girl grabs the guy's wrist, and they start fighting, rolling around in the front seat. My first thought is to run like hell and get the fuck out of there. They're wrestling for the knife. The guy is screaming at her, saying he's gonna kill her, slice her throat open. She manages to get on top of him, the knife in her hand now. He's screaming at her to stop, but she brings the knife down hard and sticks it in his shoulder.

"Now I really want to run. The guy is in pain, moaning, crying. She climbs out of the car, looks at me, and says, I am so tired of his shit. I help her drag him out of the car, the knife standing straight up out of his shoulder. He's awake and quiet. He looks sad, sitting in the dirt beside the road. The two of us climb in the car and drive away. A few miles down the road, she stops at a gas station and tells the attendant there's been an accident on the highway. The attendant asks if he should call a tow truck. Don't need a tow truck, the girl says, just an ambulance.

There's not much to say about Southern Louisiana. Flat, wet, humid, lots of oak trees dripping with Spanish moss. Dark swamps deep in the trees, wide creeks flowing slowly toward the Gulf. Everything seemed to be covered in a layer of rust or moss. Houses, cars, road signs.

Rue woke up hungry. We stopped for lunch at a barbecue shack in the small town of Welsh, Louisiana. Sitting at a picnic table under the trees, I was still amped up from the robbery. Milly looked calm.

"I want to know more about your first husband," Milly said.

Rue sighed and wiped her mouth. "It didn't end well."

"What happened?"

"I'm not going to talk about John Earl."

Milly persisted, "What did he do for a living?"

"Haven't had one of my pills since I left home," Rue said. "I feel much better, none of that awful cloudiness." She pushed her plate away. "If I start talking about John Earl, it'll just upset me."

"Fine," Milly said.

Rue opened her bag, dug out a cigarette, and lit it. Her face seemed to relax.

"John bought and sold oil leases," she said. "I met him at a fundraiser at the deaf school. He was very handsome, a wonderful speaker. The man could sell ice to Eskimos. I was at that age, about your age, when having a good-looking man turn his attention toward you, well…I began to appreciate his considerable charms. When we were courting, John pretended he didn't want anything from me. Then, after we married, he demanded everything. I quit my work with the school, and we moved south to Stringtown, Texas. It was a new oil town. I call it a town, but it was no such thing. Stringtown was a holy mess.

"Most of the town was either in tents or under construction. Cars and trucks crowded the narrow dirt streets. In dry weather, you couldn't see across the road for the clouds of dust. When it rained, the dirt roads turned into mud holes that would swallow a car. During the day, the place was a forest of wooden oil derricks blocking out the sun. Roughnecks, oil workers, and common street hoodlums roamed the town looking for whatever pleasures or corruptions were available. At night, there was no darkness. Long strings of lights were draped from derrick to derrick so work could continue at all hours. Gambling halls, bars, and cathouses roared through the night.

"We were luckier than most. John rented us a small house outside town. Not exactly a house. It was an old boxcar with a bed, a single window, and a kitchen table. At first, there seemed to be too much oil. Several wells came in all at once, and the town exploded with even more shady drifters and treasure seekers. You've never seen the like before: working girls, hustlers, con men. Farmers walked away from their property, looking to get rich in the oil business. There was no sheriff, no government. The town was too new. Oil was flowing from the ground in quantities never seen before. With so much supply, prices dropped. At one time, oil was ten cents a barrel, and a bowl of chili was fifteen cents.

"The only people making money were the crooks. I told John I wanted to leave. Stringtown was no place for us. It wasn't even a town, just a rough collection of hovels where the dregs of Texas found common ground. He wouldn't listen, saying he could smell the oil in the ground. Said one day we'd be up in a big house with lots of kids around us, money in the bank. That's how he talked, and I believed him. John was a drinker, but then everyone drank, so it didn't seem to be the problem it is these days. He'd be gone for weeks, roaming all over the county in an old Ford coupe, talking to ranchers and farmers. Making deals. My office is my back pocket, he'd tell me.

"Then after the glut came the drought. Wells stopped flowing. We'd put a lot of money into a wildcatter, and he produced nothing but dry holes. We were running out of money. John was always talking about the amount of cash moving through Stringtown. There were no banks, so money had to be trucked in every week. Cash for oil leases, money for all the bars and gambling dens. And the biggest pile was the salary for oil workers. Roughnecks all wanted to be paid in cash. John wouldn't leave it alone, talking about how a man with his talents and guile could hit the jackpot in a single night. I didn't take him seriously until I found the gun under our mattress. Whatever you're thinking about, I told him, forget it."

Rue turned to look at the clouds and took a drag on her cigarette.

"I have a few regrets in this life, not seeing my Percy more often, and being too hard on your father when he was young. But my big regret is riding into town with John that afternoon. Going along when I should have left the man. I stood there on that muddy sidewalk watching a truck pull up to a stop. Two men holding shotguns rode in the bed. A crowd of oil workers immediately surrounded the truck, and a man in a wide Stetson opened the door, climbed on the roof, and spoke to the crowd. No one goes away with empty pockets, he shouted. He pulled a list from his coat and began to call out names. The men with the shotguns opened a canvas bag and started handing out pay packets to the crowd.

"Once a man had his wages in his hand, he headed straight to the bars. Liquor, women, and gambling. A month's salary is gone in a few hours. This is wicked money, I told myself. This cash wasn't feeding homeless orphans or dropped in a collection plate. This was rum money, whore money. I told myself that under God's guidance, John and I would use this money to further the Lord's plan on Earth. Perhaps the Lord was directing our steps, putting these unlawful ideas into John's head.

"The road into Stringtown passed through a thick grove of trees where a man could stand close to the road without being seen. The morning of payday, we drove to the spot a few miles from town. John parked off the side of the road, lifted the hood, and stepped back into the trees. All I had to do was stand next to the Ford and, when the truck rolled by, wave my hand. Who could resist a young woman with car trouble?

"This isn't going to end well, is it?" Milly said.

Rue shook her head.

"The pay truck rolled by, pulled over, and stopped. John stepped out of the trees and began shooting. He winged both men riding in the bed before they could raise their shotguns. The driver stepped out, drew his pistol, and the two men went at it like outlaws, emptying their guns from close range. I fell flat to the ground when the shooting started. Smoke everywhere. I couldn't see John or the driver. All I heard was awful swearing and moaning. When the shooting stopped, I stood up and ran to John. He was hit in the stomach. The driver shot through the head. The wounded men in the truck were trying to get to their feet, reaching for their guns. I grabbed their shotguns and threw them back in the trees.

"John was in pain, bleeding badly. All he said was, Get the money. I grabbed one of the canvas bags and somehow got John to our Ford. Someone is going to drive by at any minute, I thought, and this whole fiasco will come to a proper end. But the road was empty. I turned the Ford around and drove away from Stringtown."

Rue took a deep breath. "It's a beautiful day, isn't it? We've been very fortunate with the weather..." "What happened?" Milly shouted.

"Give me a second," Rue said sharply. She held a tissue tight in her hands.

"John always kept a small watch on a chain in his vest pocket. When I had him in a hug, I could feel that watch ticking away, like a second heart. He died. Bled to death before I could get him to a doctor. I found a sandy spot near the Brazos next to a big oak tree. That's where I buried him.

Marked it with a few river rocks so I could find it later. I used to visit him now and again. Sometimes I'd bring flowers and say a few kind words over him. Then I'd spit on his grave for breaking my heart.

"What about the money?" I said.

"That's how Calvin and I bought our shoe store. So, I guess I was doing the Lord's work after all." Rue laughed. "Making sure God-fearing folks had proper footwear."

16

A few years ago, I was riding my bike into town for a Slurpee, and this dog started following me. I stopped a few times and yelled at it to go home, but it kept trotting along behind me. All the way to the 7-11. It waited for me when I went inside and sat patiently on the curb while I drank my Slurpee. I tried to pet the dog, but it moved away when I got closer. The animal followed me all the way back to my house and lay down by the back door. Never made a sound.

Our family never had pets. Dogs are too much trouble, my old man would say. And my Mother was allergic to cats, so that wasn't an option. This dog looked well-fed, wasn't dirty, and didn't bark.

When I got home from school the next day, the dog was still lying by the back door. I asked my Mother what the dog had done all day. Walked around the yard and sniffed things, she said. We didn't have any dog food, so I filled a bowl with Cap'n Crunch and set it by the back door. The dog sniffed the cereal, looked up at me, and emptied the bowl.

On my way to school the next day, I noticed a handmade poster on a telephone pole:

Lost Dog.

His name is Rex.

White with black ears.

Weighs about 25 lbs.

Reward if returned.

When I got home from school, I called the number on the sign, and a young girl answered.

"I might have your dog," I said. I described the dog and told her it had followed me home and wouldn't leave.

"That's my dog," she said.

I told her I'd been feeding him Cap'n Crunch, for the past few days.

"If you bring Rex to my house, I'll give you five dollars."

I told her I couldn't get close enough to Rex to put a leash on him.

"He doesn't like people," she said. "He only likes me."

"Then come over here and get him yourself."

"If I come over to your house, there's no reward," she said, "and you've probably made him sick feeding him that junky cereal."

"Maybe he doesn't want to go home," I said. "He's pretty happy here."

She was quiet, then said, "What if I call the police and say you stole my dog?"

"Go ahead, how are the cops gonna find me?"

There was silence.

"Meet me in the park with Rex," she said, "and I'll give you three dollars."

I imagined her being my age, and we'd fall into a relationship over her lost dog. She wasn't what I imagined and was much older than her telephone voice. I handed her the dog, and she handed me three crumpled, wet dollar bills.

The reward money gave me an idea. People were willing to pay to get their dogs back, and dogs were easy to find in my neighborhood. There were a few fences, and pets seemed to roam all over the place. Cats sleeping on front porches, dogs standing under trees barking at birds, and dogs chasing cars. I decided to grab a small one for my first theft. Easier to handle.

A small black dog was standing by the mailboxes when I rode by on my bike after school. I called it over, picked it up, and rode home. It was that easy. I didn't feel bad or guilty. I wasn't going to hurt the dog. All I wanted was a few bucks. The little dog got nervous when I got home, so I gave it a bowl of Cap'n Crunch. The animal just looked at the cereal.

I couldn't bring the dog in the house, too many questions, so I put him in the garage. Pretty soon, the dog was whining, then barking. My Mother starts walking around the house, asking where that barking is coming from. This wasn't going to work, I realized. I went out into the garage and told the dog to shut up. The dog stopped barking, happy to have company. I understood why the dog was barking, the garage was dark, and smelled like motor oil. I wouldn't have wanted to be out there alone; no wonder the animal was upset. The dog walked over and sat at my feet. What if the owner doesn't want the dog back? What if the dog is a pain in the ass and no one comes looking? It would be just my luck to grab the only unlovable dog in the whole neighborhood.

I gave the dog a pat on the head and went inside the house. My Mother was sitting in the living room, a book in her lap and a glass of wine in her hand. She wasn't reading, she was drinking. It was late afternoon, the perfect time to talk to her. She'd agree to just about anything and probably wouldn't remember what she said.

"Hey, Mom," I said. "A friend of mine asked me to keep his dog for a few days while they go out of town. Is that cool?"

"What friend?"

"You don't know him."

"What's his name?"

"Um…his name…is Frank, that's his name."

"Ok, dear," she said, "just don't make a mess."

After three days, there were no posters, and the dog was shitting and pissing all over the garage. I was afraid to take the animal out in the backyard in case someone might recognize him. Every morning before school, I'd be on my knees in the garage cleaning up the dog's business from the night before. I was so far into this thing, I couldn't turn back now.

Five days later, and still no reward posters. The dog was getting restless, chewing on old furniture and scratching deep gouges in the garage door. My father asked me how much longer the dog was going to be with us. I told him a few more days.

Why didn't I just open the garage door and let him out? Forget the whole thing. What was I thinking? I'm never sure what I'm thinking, even while I'm thinking it. Somewhere in my brain was the notion of a sizable payoff. I was stuck on the idea that the longer the dog was missing, the bigger the reward. It made sense to me at the time, so the dog stayed in the garage.

It was a rainy weekend, and the dog had been in the garage for over a week. I was in my room, and the doorbell rang. Very few people came to the door looking for me, so I ignored it. The ringing stopped, and someone was knocking. I walked downstairs and opened the door. A girl about my age was standing there. Her clothes and hair were wet. She was holding a photo.

"Have you seen my dog?"

I looked at the picture. It was the dog in my garage.

"His name is Elvis."

"How long has he been gone?"

"Almost a week. Someone might have taken him; he's very friendly."

"Why would someone take your dog?"

"I don't know," she said. "People see a nice, friendly dog and think, I'll take him home. It happens."

"I haven't seen your dog. Have you considered a reward or something? That might help." She turned to walk away.

"What's your address?" I said. "If I see Elvis, I'll bring him home."

She told me her address.

A few hours later, I knocked on her door and waited, Elvis under one arm. The door opened, and it was the girl. She let out a scream, grabbed Elvis, and ran through the living room, into the kitchen, then back into the living room. The dog was yapping happily, licking her face. The girl was laughing. I stood there watching her and Elvis doing excited laps through the house. Finally, she fell back onto the sofa out of breath, Elvis in her lap. I stepped inside.

"Thank you so much," she said. "Do you want your reward now?"

"No. That's cool. I don't need a reward."

She pushed Elvis to the floor and extended her hand.

"Sure, you do," she said.

She pulled me onto the sofa and put her arms around my neck. Then she pushed me back against the armrest and crawled on top of me. Our mouths came together. Her body was warm, her hair wet. My hands moved up and down her back. I was fifteen, not sure about anything, but I understood this immediately. I glanced down. Elvis was sitting quietly on the rug, watching.

17

"Why do people live out here?" Milly said.

She was driving now. I was riding up front. Rue was in the back reading. We were rolling through southern Louisiana. The land was flat all the way to the edge of the horizon, where it collided with a line of thick white clouds. On one side of the highway were dark, wet fields divided into sections by wire fences. A lone tractor rolled over the ground, turning up the soil. On the other side of the road was a dense green wall of pine trees. The sky looked like an immense glass bubble covering the green landscape. The Cadillac was a small chrome beetle moving slowly under the glass.

"It's probably very peaceful," I said.

"Peaceful. That's another word for boring."

"You'd prefer a city? Thousands of people, traffic."

She was quiet, thinking. "I'm not sure what's safer, hiding in the sticks or the city."

"You can't run forever."

"I'll stop running when the feds quit chasing me."

"Are you sure they're still looking for you?"

"When someone dies, they never stop hunting you."

"Change your name, cut your hair. This is a big country, you could disappear."

"You'd think so," she said, resting her chin on the steering wheel. "I was living in Phillipsburg, Montana, a while back. Beautiful little town, mountains all around. I was working as a maid in this old hotel. Had a boyfriend who worked for the Forest Service. He drove an old pickup. He was a little rough, but I liked him. He was my shelter when I really needed one. We lived in his trailer on a few acres outside town. I thought I'd found a place to hide from the mess I'd made of my life. The hotel was busy with tourists all summer, but we still had a lot of time to fish and hike. The winter was quiet and cold.

"One day, he comes in from work holding a poster he took from the post office. Three black and white images: Me, Ricky, and Greg. With big bold letters underneath: Wanted by the FBI for Interstate Flight, Murder, and Domestic Terrorism. That you? he said. I said yes, it was. Then I made the mistake of telling him everything. We had never discussed politics before, and I had assumed because we were close in age that we might have similar views about the war, about most things. I was wrong. When I stopped talking, he started pacing around the trailer. He wanted to turn me in. He said I should pay for what I did—destroying property, killing someone. It was hard to argue with him. We were trying to end the war, I said, and things went horribly wrong. He said we can't let the commies take over Vietnam, or we'll be fighting them in San Diego next. He dropped me off at the bus station the next morning, promising he wouldn't call the police.

"Do you miss him?" I asked.

"I miss Montana more than him."

We were quiet, watching the landscape roll by.

"Where's your camera?" I said.

"In my bag, why?"

"I want to take a picture."

"Of what?"

"You. You look nice right now."

I pulled the camera out of her bag, pointed it at her profile, and pushed the button. I set the picture on the dashboard in the sun and waited for the image to appear. She picked it up and looked at it. "I look tired. And I need to do something about my hair."

"You look great."

"Thanks. It's been a while since someone said that to me."

I turned to look at Rue in the backseat. She was asleep.

"I need to talk to you about something while she's asleep," I said.

Milly smiled. "My advice. Wear a condom."

"Not that. It's about something else."

I pulled the envelope from my pocket. "Got this before I left home." I unfolded the letter and read: Greetings, James Robert Birdwell. You are hereby ordered for induction into the United States Armed Forces and to report to…"

"Oh, shit."

"I have to report in three weeks."

"You don't have to do anything," she said.

"It's either report for duty or join the National Guard."

"There's always Canada or Mexico."

"My old man would disown me. Never speak to me again."

"Would that be so bad?"

"What would you do?"

"I'm doing it. Resist. Go on the run."

"I guess the war can't go on forever," I said.

"People have been saying that for years."

"If you could do things all over again, would you do it differently?"

She was quiet, then said, "The war is an atrocity; it needs to end. But if I had to do it all over, I'd be less naïve. I wouldn't be as trusting about people."

"How do you feel about God?"

"Wow. All these heavy questions."

She looked at me. I knew from her driver's license that she was only a few years older, but she was looking at me across a much greater distance.

"Yes, I believe in God," she said, "but a knowledge of God is not the same as a love of God. I'm somewhere between believing in a benevolent being and wanting this whole fucking mess to be destroyed by fire and flood. Bring on the Old Testament. Famine, war, pestilence."

"We used to go to church every Sunday," I said. "I liked the music, the singing. But the other stuff, I don't know. I didn't feel it. Too many rules and punishments. We stopped going a few years ago when the preacher did a sermon on the war. Said it was immoral. The old man stood up in the middle of the sermon and walked out."

"His business is war," she said. "He has to support it."

"Rue used to go with us. Then they remodeled the church and put in a red shag carpet. She said the place looked like a nightclub. And she stopped going." "So, what are you going to do about the letter?" I shrugged.

I had no idea what to do. The United States government is a massive machine, and refusing its commands seemed impossible. I imagined myself alone in a cold, ratty apartment in Canada, wading through deep snow to get to a minimumwage job.

We were passing through Lafayette. Milly glanced in the rearview mirror. "Oh shit."

I turned and looked out the back window. In the distance, a red flashing light was moving toward us, fast.

"You're not speeding," I said. "Just try to stay calm."

The flashing light got bigger until it was directly behind us, the siren wailing. Milly took her foot off the gas pedal, letting the Caddy gradually slow down. The cop car swerved into the left lane and flew past us.

"You ok?" I said.

"I'm fine. But we need to get off the main highway. Back roads from now on."

I turned to look at Rue. Still asleep.

"How's she doing?" Milly said.

"Once she takes her pill, that's it. She's out the rest of the afternoon."

"What's wrong with her?"

"I don't know. Some kind of heart condition. Nobody talks about anything in my family."

Milly turned off the highway at the next exit and stopped at a gas station, where I bought a map. Back on the road, I unfolded the map, tracing a meandering route across Louisiana and into Texas, avoiding the interstate, major highways, and large towns. The cop car had shaken Milly. She was quiet. She refused my offer to drive and switched on the radio. We rode in silence for miles, listening to bad country music.

Somewhere near the Texas border, we saw something strange. Milly pointed out the windshield. "What's that?"

It looked like a white cloud floating along the side of the road. As we got closer, we saw it was a young girl in a white dress running along the shoulder. She was barefoot, holding a metal container in her hands. Milly pulled up alongside her, and I rolled down my window. "Need a ride?"

The girl smiled and shook her head. "That is so kind of you." She stopped running. "The church is just up yonder." "Hop in," Milly said. "We'll give you a ride." "Well, why not?" the girl said.

She opened the back door and slid in beside Rue. Her dress was wide and full, so it took her a while to gather all the layers of the gown and pull them into the car.

"What's in the can?" Milly asked.

She lifted the urn and smiled. "Ronald Ambrose Purvis. Deceased. Obviously. I'm carrying his ashes to a memorial service at the church, and I ran out of gas." "Where's the church?" I asked.

"Just up here a ways. See that dirt road angling off to the left."

Milly put the car in drive and pressed on the gas.

"He didn't want a church service," the girl said. "He wasn't an atheist or anything. He just couldn't stand the idea of being laid in a pine box and buried in the wet ground. Having folks come by, throwing flowers on his head. Of course, Mother told him we'd do as we pleased once he passed. She said the church service wasn't for him anyway; it was for his family and friends. You know, to say good-bye.

Milly turned down the dirt road, and we saw a small white church set back in the trees. A large group of well-dressed people stood on the front lawn. The Caddy pulled to a stop. The girl jumped out, raised the urn above her head, and shouted, "Daddy's here."

The crowd broke into applause like it was a football game. The girl leaned in the window. "Y'all come inside. We'd love to have you."

Rue opened her eyes and looked around. "What in the hell is going on?"

Milly and I stood at the back of the church watching the congregation settle into the pews. The girl walked the urn to the altar, set it on a table, and took a seat in the front row. The preacher moved to the lectern and invited anyone who had something to say to step forward. The first speaker never identified herself, and it was hard to make out what she was saying through all the tears. She held a handkerchief to her face, mumbled about the deceased being the rock of the community, a true family man. Then she broke down and had to be helped back to her seat by the preacher. A young man in a suit too small for him walked to the front of the church and glared at the audience. He looked angry.

"I don't even know where to start," he said. "Ronnie was no rock of the community. He was a hound dog. Chased anything in a skirt. And he wasn't killed in a hunting accident, as they say in the papers. Man was shot while climbing out of a bedroom window."

An older man stood up from a pew in the back and yelled, "This ain't the damn time for that, son. Sit your ass down."

"I will not," the young man shouted. He opened his coat and pulled out a pistol. The crowd got very quiet.

"This is not good," Milly whispered.

The young man picked up the urn under one arm and started down the center of the church, holding the pistol at his side. "Don't nobody try to stop me."

The crowd waited until he was out of the church, then we all moved slowly out onto the lawn, curious to see what might happen. The young man set the urn down in the gravel driveway.

"This is what the cocksucker deserves," he shouted. He stepped back and emptied the pistol into the urn. The metal container bounced and rolled across the gravel. A small cloud of the dead man's ashes drifted across the road, covering the young man.

The older man who had stood up in the church stepped forward and grabbed the young man by the arm. "You happy now? What in the hell is the matter with you?" He dragged the young man to a car, pushed him inside, and drove off.

I looked up and saw Rue leaning against the Caddy, shaking her head.

We found out later that the girl in the white dress was Cora. She waited until the car drove off, then picked up the urn. There were several holes in it, and the lid didn't fit right. The stunned crowd drifted back to their cars and drove off.

Cora asked for a ride to her car to get a few things and invited us to a reception for her father at the VFW Hall in town. She sat in the backseat holding the damaged urn and looking a little overwhelmed.

Ronald had two families," she said. "Well... two that we know about. I'm the youngest from the first family. My Mother married Ronald twenty years ago and had two kids, my sister and me. Things didn't work out so well, mainly because Daddy couldn't keep his pants on, and partly because he was never sure I was his. But he couldn't divorce Momma, or he'd lose half his land. So, they came to an arrangement. It was kind of a one-sided deal. Daddy got to do whatever he wanted, and Momma got to stay home with us kids."

"Who was the guy with the gun?" I asked.

"That was Junior."

"And he's your brother?"

"Half-brother. About a year ago, we found out Daddy had a whole other family. Some woman he met down in Leesville. Put her up in a trailer. She had two kids with him. Junior is her oldest."

"He seemed pretty upset," Milly said.

"He only recently found out about us. Guess it was too much family all at once."

The car was quiet, then Cora said, "We were gonna hire a crop duster and spread his ashes over the farm. Guess Junior took care of that for us."

The VFW Hall was a low, shabby building next to a railroad crossing. The gravel parking lot was nearly full. We found a spot and climbed out of the car. Milly and Cora walked ahead, Cora still carrying the mangled urn. Rue pulled me aside. "Well, that was sure different." I nodded.

"These people are trailer trash," she said. "I'm not sure I want to go in there."

"Just one drink. Then we'll get back on the road."

My memory of that night is a little hazy. Someone handed me a beer when I stepped inside. I drank it quickly, then had several more. I recall talking to Cora for a long time, but I can't remember anything we talked about. I stood watching her mouth open and close, nodding when it seemed appropriate. The strap on her dress had slipped off her shoulder, and the dress slid down until I could see the smooth contour of her breasts. They looked very nice, and I wanted to put my hand on one of them. I must have been staring because Cora snapped her fingers and pointed to her face. "The show's up here, Jim."

Later in the evening, I moved to the buffet, thinking food might sober me up. I loaded a plate with barbecue, cornbread, and cole slaw and found an empty seat next to an older gray-haired man with an unlit cigar in his mouth.

"Who the hell are you?" he said. I started to explain the chain of events that had led to my being seated next to him, then stopped. "Friend of the family," I said.

He reached out his hand and told me his name, which I immediately forgot.

"I was the man's accountant for twenty years," he said.

"Is it true…how he died?"

He took the cigar out of his mouth. "You're not a reporter, are you?"

"No, sir."

He took a matchbook from his pocket and took his time lighting the cigar. When the tip was glowing red, he removed the cigar and said, "Ronald was shot in the chest with a small-caliber handgun and was pronounced dead at 2 a.m. You know anybody who hunts in the middle of the night with a pistol?"

I shook my head.

I couldn't eat my food. The sweet, smoky aroma of the barbecue was making me queasy. It was dark outside now. I looked around the room for Milly and Rue. Rue had a drink in her hand and was talking to a man who looked like he spent a lot of time outside. His sleeves were rolled up to his elbows, and he had thick brown forearms.

A band set up in the corner and started playing slow country music. A few couples shuffled around the dance floor. I had to get some fresh air. I was feeling sick.

I stumbled outside, climbed in the back of the Cadillac, and closed my eyes. A few hours later or a few minutes later, I can't be certain, the car door opened, the dome light came on, and Milly and Cora slid into the front seat.

"We're going on a midnight adventure," Cora said. "And you're coming with us." She sounded drunk.

Milly started the car and backed out onto the road.

"Where are we going?" I said. "We can't leave Rue."

"She found a friend," Milly said. "She'll be fine."

"Mother always says nothing good happens after midnight," Cora said.

"Well, she's wrong."

Cora pulled a joint from somewhere and lit the end, handing it to Milly, who took a puff and handed it back. They passed the joint back and forth, ignoring me.

"Aren't you gonna share?"

Milly laughed. "What would your old man say?"

"He's not here, so fuck him." I grabbed the joint and took a long drag.

Cora slid close to Milly and put her arm around her, playing with her hair.

"I like boys when I'm sober," Cora said, "and girls when I'm drunk."

We rolled down empty back roads through dark green fields. The deep hum of the Cadillac moving over the pavement made it feel like the car was floating over the ground. A wide channel of stars filled the sky above the trees. We seemed to be going deeper into the countryside, further away from houses and people and rules.

The Caddy rolled to a stop at a metal gate. Cora jumped out, swung the gate open, and we motored through. Several cars were parked outside an old barn where a small crowd stood around a fire. When we climbed out of the car, someone said Cora's name. She waved to a few people as the crowd moved slowly toward the barn.

Inside, we gathered around a large horse stall. It was quiet. Everyone seemed to be waiting for something to happen, for someone to arrive. A man stepped through the barn door into the faint light, leading a large black dog on a leash. The leash wrapped tight around his wrist. Another man entered the barn, restraining a stocky gray dog. The instant the animals saw each other, they jumped hard against their leashes, leaping in the air, growling, neck muscles bulging. The two men struggled to control the dogs.

A man in a battered cowboy hat climbed to the top rail of the stall, waving a stack of money. "Let me hear it," he yelled to the crowd.

People began shouting the names of the dogs, pushing cash at the man. He grabbed the money, shouting out names and amounts. The two owners led the dogs into the stall. When all the bets were down, the man in the cowboy hat nodded. The two men dropped their leashes, scrambling to the top rail. The dogs slammed into each other, a sickening collision of muscle and bone. Jaws wide, drooling, snapping. They stood on their back legs, roaring at each other, then crashing to the ground. The black dog sank its teeth into the gray dog's thick neck. The gray dog was clawing and snapping to get free. Milly stood beside me, looking through a gap in the boards. She was breathing heavily. Cora sat on the top rail, holding a beer. She was shouting something, but I couldn't hear over the howling dogs. Red, screaming faces peered through the wooden slats.

The dogs stood up abruptly and backed away from each other. The gray dog had most of one ear missing, blood streaming from a ragged gash. The black dog had a deep wound in its chest. Both animals stood panting, heads down, quietly eyeing each other.

"Ain't over till it's over," the man in the cowboy hat yelled.

"This is bullshit," someone yelled. "We come to see a fight."

Someone threw a beer bottle. It shattered against the boards. The handlers climbed into the stall, leaned close, and spoke to their dogs. Dragging their dogs to the center of the stall, the handlers dropped their grip on the collars and jumped back. The two animals stood quietly for a few seconds, breathing hard, and then the black dog charged forward, jumped on the gray dog's back, and sank its teeth deep into its neck. There was a sharp wail, and the gray dog fell to the ground and rolled on its back. The black dog stood over its opponent, tearing at its throat. Blood sprayed across the stall, across the faces of the howling crowd. The man in the cowboy hat jumped down into the stall, waving his hat. It was over. I'd seen enough. I turned and walked out of the barn.

On the ride back to the VFW Hall, Milly and Cora decided that Cora was going to Texas with us.

"Both families will be circling Daddy's will like vultures," Cora said. "I don't want any part of it. Ronald had a lot of money, a lot of land. He's got two families to satisfy. I just hope he carves out a little cash for me."

"You're his daughter," Milly said. "That's worth something."

"You'd think so. But there are things about me that Ronald didn't like."

"Like what?" I said.

"Sometime in the past, one of my white ancestors was canoodling with the dark races. That's where my kinky hair and less than lily-white skin come from."

"And you think Ronald will cut you out of the will for that?" Milly said.

"I was an embarrassment to him. Maybe he wants to punish me and Mother one more time. It's something he'd do."

When we got back to the VFW Hall, there were only a few cars in the parking lot. We found Rue asleep across some chairs in the main room. An older couple was slow dancing even though there was no music. I helped Rue back to the Caddy, and we drove to Cora's place.

She lived in one of those fake Southern plantation homes with tall white pillars and a line of trees arching over a long driveway. We parked out front, and Cora ran inside, still carrying the wounded urn. A light went on in an upstairs room. I looked in the backseat to see if Rue was still awake.

"If I'm gonna stay up all night," she said, "I could use a drink."

"I think I drank myself sober," Milly said.

The porch light went on, and a woman stepped out of the door and walked over to the car. I assumed it was Cora's mom. She leaned in the driver's window, trying to see who was inside. Her face is tight.

"We're sorry for your loss, ma'am," Rue said.

"Not sure if it's a loss or a relief. That man was exhausting. Lived every minute like it was his last one."

She turned to see Cora coming out of the house with a bag. "I don't know you folks, and I can't tell my daughter not to go, but please look after her for me." "We will, ma'am," Milly said.

I climbed over the seat, and Cora slid in next to Milly. As we drove away, Cora's mom raised her hand slowly in a tentative wave.

18

Why does the world seem so big at night? And all your troubles seem so far away? It felt like we were all alone, drifting through space. A dark sky overhead, seeded with a wide field of stars. The Caddy's illuminated chrome dashboard looked like the controls of a spaceship, telling us everything we needed to track our progress: time, speed, distance.

We cruised through a series of small towns: Dry Creek, Sugartown, Rose Pine. Nobody was sleepy. We had all reached that point in the night where the body craves stimulation rather than rest. Milly found an all-night liquor store, bought a pint of Wild Turkey, and we passed it back and forth while Cora talked about her father.

"We have a fish camp over on Lake Hatch. It's this little shack on pillars deep in the trees. Mother hates the place. There's no electricity or running water, and everything is moldy and damp. Ronald built a long wooden pier off the front and kept an old flat-bottom fishing boat tied up at the dock. He'd take his buddies down there to drink and play poker. They never brought back any fish. Once in a while, he would ask me to go with him. I liked it down there, all the birds, miles from anything. The silence was amazing. Ronald seemed to soften a little while he was there. He was content to sit on the dock, drink beer, play gin rummy, and listen to the radio. It was just Ronald and me.

"One time, as we were walking out the door, Mother asked us to look after her dog Ziggy for the weekend. She had one of those little Chihuahuas. Ronald tried to tell her the camp was no place for a dog, but she insisted. When we got to the camp, Ronald said, " No matter what, don't let the damn dog out of the shack. It'll fall into the water and drown, and your Mother will skin me.

"It was a terrible weekend, cold and cloudy. Ronald and I spent most of the time inside playing cards and watching Ziggy. Sunday morning, the sun came out, so we took chairs outside and walked to the end of the pier and sat down. I guess we left the screen door open because when we looked back, Ziggy was walking toward us, down the dock. Ronald yelled at the dog to get back inside, but Ziggy kept coming. The little dog stopped and sniffed the air. And then something exploded out of the water. An alligator erupted from under the surface, scrambled onto the pier, snatched the dog in its jaws, and slid back into the water. Ronald and I were too stunned to move. The surface of the lake was barely disturbed, just a few ripples where the gator had slipped quietly back under the water. We told Mother that Ziggy had run off. Neither one of us would have been able to tell her the truth with a straight face.

"It's those kinds of things that drive couples apart," Rue said, shaking her head.

"You can't really split up a marriage that was never together," Cora said. "I don't think Ronald ever got over the war. He called it the good war. Said it was the last time this country was in a fight that could be morally justified. They put a rifle in his hands and told him to kill Germans. He'd never had so much fun. He never recovered from all the excitement. For the rest of his life, adrenaline was his drug. Women, gambling, booze, fast cars. He was a terrible father, an awful role model, and the most fun I've ever had."

Cora looked out the window. "He cheated on her from day one. Didn't even try to hide it. It's a wonder he lived so long."

Milly took a sip from the bottle. "How did he make his money?"

"He won ten acres in a poker game, and then he traded, swapped, and bartered. He was good at that, hustling, making deals. And he was lucky most of his life. Until he wasn't."

Even in the dim light, I could see that Cora was close to tears.

"He took me to Vegas on my eighteenth birthday. Lord, what was he thinking? He worked his way through the casinos, gambling, smoking cigars, and picking up women. The only thing I wanted for my birthday was to know who my father was. I knew it wasn't him. Ronald and Mother had this fucked up pact. Neither one would say who my Daddy was. His lawyer told me that in his will, Ronald named my father. But fuck them both. I already know who he is. I went to school with this girl whose momma was the nurse on duty when I was born. Her Mother said she got a call at the hospital. A man wanted to know if Mrs. Purvis and the child were ok. The nurse told him yes, everything was fine, and could she ask who was calling? The man thanked her, said his name, and hung up.

"Who was it?" Milly asked.

"A man named Walter Rudy lives down south near
Avery Island."

"So, you've met him?"

"No. I hired an investigator to find out a little more about him. He's a big man down there. Owns a ranch and a few businesses. He's Cajun, so that explains a lot about my appearance."

The car was quiet, then Rue said, "We don't get to choose our family. All we can do is try to survive them."

Cora took a sip. "When I heard my father was dead, I asked God for some advice, a little guidance perhaps. As usual, I heard nothing."

We were all quiet until Milly snapped on the radio and found a jazz station out of New Orleans. The Caddy rolled down the dark, empty highway. I leaned back and looked at the night sky through the back window. Cora handed the bottle to Rue, and she took a sip.

"This was back in 1930, or '31," Rue began. "Banks were failing. Your money wasn't safe. Jobs were scarce, and Texas was in the middle of a drought. We owned a

shoe store, but few folks could afford new shoes. The business wasn't looking good. I still had some of the money from Stringtown, but Calvin didn't know anything about it. He thought the money I'd given him for the store was what I'd inherited from my father. We'd been married for a few years, and I wanted to be a good wife. So, like a little fool, I told him about the money. Three Mason jars filled with cash, the lids sealed with wax and buried in the garden. Calvin didn't know what to say. His Christian side said we should give the money back. Give it back to who? I said. They'll drag me to
Huntsville the minute I tell my story.

"He said he'd have to pray about it. He mulled it over for a few days, and after considerable thought, his business side took over. He said as long as we used the money for good, we could keep it.

"Calvin said paper money is worthless. We need to convert this cash into gold or silver, and the best place to do that is Mexico. As hard as the Depression hit this country, Mexico got it worse. But one thing Mexico never ran short of was gold and silver. Calvin said it would be simple. We drive down to Monterrey, exchange the paper money for gold coins, and drive home. We can do it over a weekend.

"I didn't create my life from good Christian choices. I threw it together with whatever careless circumstances came my way. And often I didn't recognize a good decision from a bad one until a lot of water was under the bridge. That spring was hot and dry. We crossed the border at Laredo in the early afternoon and motored south. We could see the blue mountains of the Sierra Madre in the distance. The land across the border looked a lot like Texas. Flat, dry, and poor. Except for a few old rusted coupes, overloaded trucks, and donkey carts, the highway was nearly empty. I had convinced Calvin to bring a pistol along, an old six-shot Smith & Wesson I used around the house for snakes and coyotes. But it wasn't loaded, and the bullets were in Calvin's pocket. I should have been carrying the weapon, but Calvin wouldn't have it. The man had strange notions about women and guns.

"We stopped at a dusty crossroad to fill up with gas. A woman stood outside a hut tending a cooking fire. The houses were simple shacks, wooden stakes lashed together for walls, and matted grass for a roof. We ate warm tortillas, watching the light fading from the sky.

"Before I left the house, I packed the money into a small leather bag. The bag had been resting on my lap the entire trip, with both hands gripping the handle. I was trying to stay calm, but the amount of money we were carrying made me nervous. I'd been to Mexico a few times with my father, crossing at Acuna, but never going more than a few miles from the border. This was different. This journey was like traveling backward in time. There were no road signs, no maps. Calvin spoke no Spanish, and I had only a few words.

"The sun was down when we rolled into Monterrey. Calvin was tired from the drive and needed a rest. I wanted to walk around and look at the city. He wouldn't have it, so we argued. Calvin was a good man, honest, trustworthy, but he'd been raised with a set of childish beliefs about marriage, ideas that were old even then. I married him because I needed a safe place to rest. I suppose it's never too late to seek a second life. When he was tired of shouting, he lay on the bed and closed his eyes. I waited until he fell asleep, locked the door behind me, and stepped out into the city. Crossing a busy street, I wandered through a park, nodding at families and women pushing prams, young children running ahead. I bought a scoop of ice cream from a street vendor, sat on a park bench, and watched these ordinary lives. My nervousness seemed to fade. I walked back to the hotel and found Calvin asleep. I took the pistol from his bag and loaded it, just in case.

"The next morning, we checked out early and drove around the city looking for a bank. We were standing at the door of Banco Segura when a guard unlocked it and let us inside. The young lady who helped us spoke English, but after Calvin explained what we wanted, she shook her head and said it was not possible. She called over her manager, who explained that changing American dollars for gold and silver coins was legal only at government-approved locations. He wrote down an address, 213 Calle Violeta, and handed it to Calvin.

"We drove through Monterrey for hours. There seemed to be no rational pattern to the addresses and very few street signs. It was late in the day, and we didn't want to spend another night in Monterrey. Finally, I told Calvin to park the car. We climbed out and walked slowly along the street until we found the address. It was hidden between two houses, set back from the road behind a tall fence. I rang the bell at the gate, and we waited. After several minutes, an older man stepped out on the porch to see who was at his gate.

Dinero para cambiar, I said. He nodded and let us inside.

"The interior of his house resembled a jail with iron bars over the windows and doors, and thick metal rods from ceiling to floor dividing the room. He motioned to a table and chairs, and we sat down. Calvin opened the bag and set the cash in front of the old man.

We want to exchange this for gold, he said.

Cuanto en la bolsa? the old man asked.

Tres mil dolares americanos, I said.

He stood up, walked to a steel cabinet, opened it, and pulled out a canvas sack. He emptied it on the table. Even in the dim room, the bright gold coins glowed like little suns.

I thought Calvin might faint. He picked up a coin, rubbing it between his fingers.

How pure is it? Calvin asked.

We will test, the old man said. He took a medicine bottle from his pocket. Vinagre, he said, and put a small drop on the coin. We all stared at the coin, waiting. Nothing happened.

Clear is good, the old man said. If cloudy, it is impure.

"Calvin extended his hand, and the old man shook it. Let's do some business, Calvin said. The old man went to the cabinet and pulled out a set of ancient brass scales. Scribbling on the back of an envelope, he came up with a figure and then pushed the envelope at Calvin.

"Show me in coins," Calvin said. The old man made three neat stacks, each with five gold coins, and a fourth stack with half a dozen silver coins. I picked up one of the gold coins. On one side was the date, 1866. On the other side, the profile of Emperor Maximilian. Calvin was nodding. I could tell he was pleased. The old man picked up two silver coins, rolling them in his hand. They rang like tiny bells. The sound of money, the old man said.

"The old man had given us a small pouch for the coins. I held it tight in my hand. I wasn't going to let it out of my grasp until we crossed back into Texas. Calvin was feeling good, satisfied with himself, talking about what he might do with the money. Open another shoe store. Dallas would be a good location, he said. Or buy some acreage. Land is always a good investment; they're not making any more of it.

"We were on an empty stretch of road, miles south of Laredo, heading home. Nothing but sand, sage, and flat, barren desert. Up ahead, an old truck blocked the highway. As we got closer, we saw a man standing behind the truck, waving us down. I felt something was wrong and reached into my bag for the pistol. I told Calvin not to stop, just drive around him.

Ridiculous, he said. The man might need some assistance.

Calvin pulled to a stop, and the Mexican walked over. Buenos tardes, he said.

Calvin nodded.

I noticed your license plate from Texas. I have a cousin who lives in the north, perhaps you know him?

It's a big country, Calvin said.

Yes, very big. His name is Felipe Molina. He lives in Chicago.

I don't believe I know him, Calvin said.

The man shrugged and looked away.

Do you need some help? Calvin asked.

The man leaned in the window. No, he said, I stop to collect tax.

The man wore a leather holster and a pistol.

I pushed the gun deeper into the folds of my dress.

What tax? Calvin said.

Road tax.

That's news to me.

Yes… is big surprise for everyone, the man said.

Cuanto? I said.

The man put his hand on the butt of his pistol and looked at me.

Everything, señora.

I waited for Calvin to say something. He was quiet. He looked confused.

It's in the trunk, I said. I'll show you. I opened the door and stepped out. Calvin tried to grab my arm and pull me back, but I was out and moving toward the trunk. As the Mexican walked around the back of the Ford, I leveled the pistol at his stomach. He smiled at me.

How many men you killed, señora?

You'll be my first, I said. I was calm.

For me, too many to count, he said.

Drop your pistol on the ground.

Si señora. He lifted the pistol out of the holster and dropped it on the ground.

Now walk. And if you do anything silly, I'll shoot you.

Yes. I believe you will.

We walked out into the desert. The setting sun had turned the sky a vivid red.

The man asked if I was going to kill him.

I don't think so, I said.

That is good, he said. He was worried that if he were gone from the earth, no one would care for his wife and children. I watched him move slowly across the sand until his dark figure was small against the sky. Then I turned, ran back to the road, and put three holes in the truck's radiator.

"Calvin wouldn't look at me when I climbed in beside him. We rode in silence to the border and back home. Our marriage was never the same after that."

19

We crossed the Sabine River and rolled into Texas just as the sun was coming up. East Texas looked a lot like Louisiana, deep grassy fields dotted with grazing cows. Dense stands of pine trees. Milly was driving. Rue and Cora were asleep in the back seat. We'd finished the pint hours ago, and now, with the light returning to the sky, I was thinking about breakfast. I unfolded the map to find our location. We were a few miles from Kirbyville, Texas, and about 350 miles from Utopia. If the wheels didn't fall off the Caddy, we'd be in Utopia by lunch.

I asked Milly if she wanted me to drive. She had been behind the wheel for several hours. She shook her head. The highway was empty, only a few farm trucks pulling trailers loaded with hay. A muddy pickup raced up in the left lane to pass the Caddy, then slowed down, coming alongside us. The guy in the passenger seat pulled his pants down and pressed his butt to the glass, then turned and waved at us. The truck accelerated up the road.

"Rednecks," Milly said. "They're everywhere."

We stopped in Kirbyville for coffee and donuts and sat in the car watching the town wake up. Pickup trucks rolling down Main Street, lights going on in a hardware store, and a gas station. It was another slow Saturday morning in a sleepy little Texas town.

Back out on the highway. Green fields, trees, and a blazing sunset in a monotonous blue sky. It was hard to keep my eyes open. I leaned against the door, the morning sun warming the car. I was about to nod off when Milly shook me awake.

"What?" I said.

"You need to stay awake so you can keep me awake."

"How do I keep you awake when I'm falling asleep?"

"Talk to me. Tell me something about yourself."

I looked at her. "There's not much to tell. My whole fucking life comes down to what I'm gonna do about that letter. Do I run or do I join up?"

"Flip a coin. Let the universe decide."

"I don't think I'd make a good soldier."

She laughed. "You'd be the perfect soldier. You've been training with your old man your whole life." I looked at her grinning face.

"How long has it been since you've seen your family?" I asked.

"Awhile." She put a hand through her hair. "I called them once a few months after the…incident, trying to explain what happened. It didn't go well. With my parents, you're either for the war or against it; there's no middle ground."

"After you left school, you went to California, right?"

"Yeah. Before he left town, Ricky gave me the name of this guy who lived in Sausalito on a houseboat. He said the guy would find me a safe place to hide out. I was in a bad way, leaving everything behind, not sure of my next move. The FBI is after me. So, I called the guy up, and he met me in a coffee shop. Ruben was the name he gave me. He seemed okay. He'd been to Vietnam. Talked a lot about the struggle, how this fight was just the beginning. He asked me if I was ready for years of armed conflict with the power structure. I'd been on a bus for twenty hours. I was hungry, scared, and dirty, and all I wanted was a hot shower and a long sleep. So, I decided to roll the dice and trust this guy. Doesn't matter how many good choices or bad choices you make in life; luck always has the last word.

"He lived on a houseboat with a bunch of people. It was this floating revolutionary circus. I don't know how many people lived there; they came and went at all hours, slept on the floor, sunned on the deck, drank, smoked, fucked, and talked. If they were awake, they were talking about how to end the war, how to address the race question, how to bring down the system. I found a vacant corner in a room with two other people. Nobody introduced themselves; it didn't matter since everyone had a false name, a nom de guerre. I tried to lay low, tried to make myself invisible. For the longest time, I dreamed about getting my old life back. Changing my name, finding a job, and going back to school. I wanted to end the war, but I didn't want it to fuck up my whole life."

She paused. "It's the small acts of denial that keep life going. I was delusional. I was on the run from the FBI, and I was dreaming about a nice little home in the suburbs." "It could still happen," I said.

Milly stared at me with what looked like pity and amusement. "I guess you haven't been paying attention. The world is on fire. Our country is a holy, fucking mess. Things don't work anymore; everything's broken. The whole system is staggering to its death, which gives people permission to live their lives in chaos, with no rules. I'm glad the old world is dying, there's not much that deserves to be saved, but I'm frightened of what the new world will look like."

We were quiet. The low rumble of the engine filled the car.

"Can I drive if you want?" I said.

"I'm fine. Too wired to sleep. What were we talking about?"

"California."

She took a deep breath and exhaled. "I started hanging out with this guy on the houseboat. Said his name was Luis. His Mother was Puerto Rican and lived in Miami. He was AWOL from basic training. Not sure if any of it was true, but that was his story. He'd been on the houseboat for six months. He had a job as a chef in San Francisco. I was lonely, I needed a warm body next to me, someone to hang on to.

Sex with him was pretty plain, but his food was fantastic. The man could cook. Luis was a nice guy, but he had no idea what to do next, no plan. He was a follower. When Ruben started talking about making a political statement, I knew what that meant. They wanted to plant a bomb somewhere. I'd told Luis in secret about my past, how a bomb is a terrible idea, but I guess there are no secrets in a revolution. He went straight to Ruben and told him I was an expert with bombs.

"Ruben came to me with the idea of putting a bomb in the lobby of Bank of America in San Francisco, then calling it in to the police and telling them the device would explode in fifteen minutes. Everyone would be evacuated, and we'd release a statement. What kind of statement? I said. A communique, he said, we would let the world know we can strike at the heart of their fascist institutions. Ruben already had the dynamite, the detonators, the timing device, and a booklet he found at a second-hand bookstore on how to assemble a bomb. I told him I wouldn't be much help since I was just the getaway driver. In my head, I'm thinking, how do I get away from these crazy fuckers? I hadn't been able to find a job, and I was down to my last few bucks. I made the mistake of asking Luis for some money, which made him suspicious, and he went to Ruben. After that, they thought I was an informer, working for the pigs. Everyone was paranoid back then. Ruben locked me in a storage room and had someone watch me.

"The bombing was scheduled for the Friday before Labor Day. Luis was supposed to drive the bomb into town, park the car, switch to a taxi, then leave the bomb in the lobby of the bank at exactly one in the afternoon. Ruben had set the timer for 1:15. Plenty of time for Luis to get clear of the building. At the last minute, Ruben decided that I should go with Luis, so he could keep an eye on me. They were afraid I might call the cops or something. I didn't give a shit about their political statements or communiques; I just wanted to get away from those weirdos.

"Ruben, let me read the communique. It was ridiculous:

Freaks are revolutionaries and revolutionaries are freaks. We're kids making love, smoking dope, and loading guns, fugitives from American justice...

"The whole thing sounded like it was written by a high school student. Friday morning, Luis and I drove across the bridge into the city. A leather briefcase with six sticks of dynamite was sitting on my lap. I was thinking about where to go once this stupidity was over with. I had seventeen dollars and change in my pocket. We stopped at a coffee shop and had breakfast. Luis was nervous, looking at his watch and the briefcase next to his chair. We walked around Nob Hill, killing time. When it was close to one o'clock, we grabbed a cab and gave the driver the address: 555 California St., in the financial district. Traffic was light. It was a beautiful day, clear blue sky, the smell of the ocean in the air. The cab turned down Pine St., and the road was jammed with protesters. Hundreds of people are chanting and holding signs. It was some kind of Teamsters demonstration. Cars were coming to a stop behind us. We couldn't go forward or back. The cabbie looked at us, asked if we were in a hurry, and said this could take a while.

"Luis asked how far to the Bank of America. Maybe eight blocks, the driver says. Luis looked at his watch. Thirteen minutes to one, he says. I told him we'd never make it. Luis was screaming in Spanish now. He opened the door and jumped out, trying to push his way through the crowd. I told the driver to hang on, I'd be right back. I followed Luis through the screaming crowd. He was standing in the middle of the street, frozen, holding the briefcase to his chest.

"Let's go, I said, we've got to go. He shook his head. Then give me the bag, I said. He hugged the briefcase tighter. I turned to walk away, then slugged him in the face as hard as I could. He didn't see it coming. I think I broke something in my hand. I grabbed the bag and ran back to the taxi. What's the fastest way to the water? I said. The cabbie shrugged. There's a bomb in here, I said, and it'll go off in about eight minutes. We need to get to the Embarcadero.

"The demonstration was thinning out now. The driver ran the taxi up on the sidewalk and drove down Broadway. I could see the blue water in the distance. I screamed at him, Just go, go. We ran all the red lights until we hit the Embarcadero. I thought maybe I could throw the bag off the bridge, but the bridge was another mile south. We'd never make it. Is there a pier or some way to get out over the water? I said. There's a short pier at the ferry building, he said. What time is it? I said. It was ten after one. When we got to the ferry building, I jumped out, ran through the building, and out onto the pier. A ferry was pulling away from the dock. I ran to the rail, heaved the briefcase out over the water, turned and ran as fast as I've ever run."

Milly was quiet.

"What happened?"

"Nothing. I guess the saltwater messed up the detonator, or Ruben didn't know what the fuck he was doing."

20

Junction City, Kansas, was one of the whitest places we ever lived. There were a few Mexican families working in the meat processing plant outside town, but they mostly kept to themselves. And there were even fewer Black people. Posey Banks was the only Black kid in my homeroom class. We both sat in the back of the room as far away from the teacher as possible. Once in a while, we would talk. I don't remember what we talked about, except for this one day. Posey came in late, and the teacher asked him if he had an excuse. Posey made a face and grabbed his crotch. The teacher ignored him, and Posey walked to his desk and sat down. I looked over at him.

"What are you looking at?" Posey said.

I was a little afraid of him. He was short but had thick muscles across his shoulders and arms.

"Man fussing at me on the bus this morning," he said. "Had to set him straight."

"What happened?"

"Showed him the shooter I was carrying. Didn't say anything after that."

"You don't have a gun," I said. "Where would you get a gun?"

He glared at me. "The fuck you talking about…damn right I got a gun." "Show it to me."

He shook his head.

I wouldn't let it go. "You don't have a gun. You're too young to buy a gun, even in Kansas."

He pulled his desk closer and looked at me. He was trying to decide if I was stupid or insane. "You're ignorant," he said, smiling. "Gonna get you in trouble."

"If you have a gun, show it to me."

"Wanna see my gun?" He grabbed his dick and laughed.
"I show you my gun."

"I knew you were bullshitting. There's no gun."

He leaned close. "You don't shut your face…I'll show you my motherfucking gun."

"You're full of shit."

The bell rang to end homeroom. Posey stood up and pointed at me. "Tomorrow morning, in front of the school." And walked out.

The next morning, I was waiting near the front doors. I saw Posey walking toward me, carrying a small backpack. He pointed toward the teacher's parking lot. I followed him.

There was a tall, thick hedge along the side of the building. Posey ducked behind the hedge and disappeared. I followed. He was crouched on the ground, holding the backpack. He unzipped it and held it open. Inside was a large black pistol with a wooden grip. Posey grabbed the gun and pushed it against my chest.

"You open your mouth, I put a big hole in you.
Understand?"

Too scared to speak, I nodded.

"Now get the fuck outta here."

Somewhere near Cut and Shoot, Texas, we got stuck behind a truck pulling a trailer stacked with hay. Milly couldn't see the road ahead to pass, so we were doing twenty miles an hour, waiting for the truck to turn off the highway. The sun was high in the sky, the glare sharp across the windshield.

Sunglasses, I thought. When we stop for gas, I'll get a pair of cheap sunglasses.

Cora and Rue were asleep in the backseat.

The truck finally turned off the highway, and Milly increased her speed. As we approached a crossroad, I saw a car coming fast down a dirt road toward the intersection. Clouds of dust trailed the car.

"Is that guy gonna stop?" Milly said.

The car kept coming, ignoring the stop sign, sliding out onto the highway. Milly turned sharply, trying to avoid the car, but it was too late. The Caddy slammed into the vehicle, sending it spinning off the highway into the grass. Milly was calm, letting the Caddy roll to a stop at the side of the road. I opened the door and looked back at the car, nearly buried in the tall weeds and grass. The driver was standing next to the car, looking at the damage. He seemed okay. One side of his car was crushed, the windows smashed.

Milly and I climbed out and walked toward the driver. "You ok, man?"

The driver looked up and grabbed a small gym bag from the back seat. He was wearing a dirty white dress shirt, jeans, and no shoes. He looked like he'd dressed in a hurry and forgotten a few things. His glasses sat crookedly on his face.

"This is embarrassing," he said.

"Don't worry about it," Milly said. "I'm glad you're alright."

"Well. I'm about as far from alright as a man can be." He unzipped the bag and pulled out a small pistol, holding it casually at his side. "I need your vehicle. I have to be someplace this afternoon."

Cora and Rue were out of the car now, walking toward us.

"Don't you want to do something about your car?" Milly said. She pointed to the wrecked vehicle, smoke coming from under the hood.

"It's not my car. I stole it this morning." We were all quiet, thinking about that.

Then Rue said, "Are you some kind of outlaw?"

He smiled. "Oh, no, ma'am, I'm a high school science teacher." He looked at the four of us. "Are you a family or something?"

"My name is LaRue Birdwell, and this is my grandson, Jim. These other two..." She shook her head.

"We should call a tow truck and get a police report," I said. As soon as the words were out of my mouth, I knew it was the wrong thing to say.

"No police," Milly said.

He waved the gun at Milly. "We're all going to get back in the Cadillac, and this young lady is going to drive me where I need to go, so I can deliver this package. Is that all right, Miss Birdwell?"

"Do I have a choice?" Rue said.

I walked back to the Cadillac to check out the damage. A thick, chrome bumper protected the front end of the Caddy. Above the bumper was a metal grill that looked like a set of silver teeth. The only damage was a small scrape on the bumper. The Caddy was a tank, nearly indestructible.

Milly slid behind the wheel. Rue, Cora, and I climbed into the back seat. The man with the gun sat up front. She eased out onto the empty blacktop and accelerated up the road.

"If you're going to steal my vehicle," Rue said, "the least you can do is introduce yourself."

"I am so sorry, ma'am. Got in a big hurry, forgot all my manners." He turned to look at Rue. "My name is Troy Higbee. Pleased to meet you."

"And where are we going, Mr. Higbee?" Rue said.

"Houston."

From the time Troy Higbee climbed into the Caddy, he never closed his mouth. He was a compulsive talker, but he never talked about anything interesting. He'd ramble on about his life and family, but his stories never went anywhere. His voice would dwindle to inaudible mumbles. Then he'd take a deep breath and start off on another long-winded episode. It didn't seem to matter that no one was listening.

All I wanted to know was what was in the bag and why he'd stolen a car. And he made me nervous the way he held the gun. The pistol was loose in his grip, the barrel swinging wildly back and forth.

Finally, Milly spoke up. "Can you not wave that thing around? You're making me jumpy."

Troy set the gun down on the center console and started another story. "My father was a preacher for a short time. A violent disaster directed him to his calling. The Lord's ways are a mystery to us. It was May 1950. He was a passenger on a streetcar in Chicago, on his way to a job interview. The streetcar ran through a red switch and plowed into a gasoline truck. Boom. The explosion broke windows miles away. The fireball roared backward from the truck, engulfing the streetcar. My father happened to be seated at the back, next to an emergency door. He jumped to his feet, opened the door, and escorted several passengers to safety. Sadly, dozens died. My father was transformed by the incident. He saw the hand of God in his survival and those of a few lucky passengers. Afterward, he sued the Chicago Transit Authority and received a check for several thousand dollars. That's how we were able to move to Texas, where he began his ministry. The Church of the Honest-to-God Truth."

I looked over at Rue, asleep against the door. Cora was staring out the window.

"Eventually, he gave up on God and burned all his sermons on the front lawn. My father only saw the Lord's handiwork when something profitable came his way. If he lost money, it was the Devil's hand. Now that we are out of the Jesus business, my Mother asked him, " How are we gonna make the house payment now? My father was a very persuasive man, but for years, he struggled to find the right game. In desperation, he turned his skills to peddling encyclopedias door-to-door. Did fairly well. It might surprise you how many folks buy a set of encyclopedias and can't even read. He found out quickly that selling books in Texas is a losing proposition. Most folks know how to read; they just prefer not to. Why sit down with a book when there's TV?"

Milly looked at Troy. "Houston's a big city. You got an address?"

"It's not a house, it's a park. I'm meeting someone there. I give him the bag, and he gives me the money. I hope."

"Then what?"

Troy looked out the window. "I don't know. I haven't thought that far ahead."

We were heading west on Highway 90. In the distance, a thick layer of smog hung over the horizon, and above the smog, a dull blue sky. Pump jacks nodded up and down in the fields. There were fewer open pastures now, more highways and roads, more strip malls and parking lots. Houston's dark outline was visible in the distance.

Troy was talking again. "We didn't have a television when I was growing up because my old man thought the Jews and the Communists controlled the airwaves. He finally bought one a few days before his alma mater, the University of Texas, played Alabama in the 1965 Orange Bowl. He stood up in front of this big Zenith console the whole game with a Scotch in his hand, screaming at the television. Passed out on the floor in the third quarter and didn't see the end of the game. Texas won."

Rue was awake now, leaning over the seat, looking at Troy.

"I'm a little worried about this whole thing," she said. "You seem like a nice fella. But the gun worries me.

People who carry guns are not always the folks who should have them."

Troy nodded. "I don't like guns either, ma'am. But without a gun, I tend to get overlooked. I don't like to be ignored. Makes me angry."

"Nobody is ignoring you," Milly said.

Troy picked up the gun and set it in his lap. "If this exchange goes well, I promise I will put this weapon down and never pick it up again. I won't need it because Ivy and I are leaving this country." "Who's Ivy?" I said.

"She's my sweetheart. Last semester, she sat in the back row of my class. I pretty much ignored her for most of the year. When she asked me for extra help, I offered to come to her house. She said no. I suppose she was ashamed of where she lived. But I got nothing against trailers. I lived in one for a while. Found out later it was her brother she was ashamed of, well, not ashamed, more like scared of. He sells weed at the high school. That was his car you folks ran into. This is his gun.

"At first, I didn't know what was going on with me. I began to feel funny. Achy head, cloudy thinking, sweaty hands. I concluded it was either the flu or I was in love. I thought perhaps the difference in our ages was too big an obstacle. I'm thirty-two, and Ivy is sixteen. Then I said, Hang on a second. Age is nothing but a number. Love doesn't count years. Finally, I talked to her after class one day. Told her how I was feeling, and it turned out she felt the same way. I was worried, however, that as I got older, her passion for me might cool. She laughed. Of course, my passion will cool, she said, but your money will keep the pot boiling. I told her I didn't have any money. She just smiled and said, I'll take care of that."

Brewster Park is on the corner of Brewster and Sumpter in the Fifth Ward. Interstate 69 runs along one side of the park, and on the other side is a railroad track. It's a small neighborhood park with swing sets, slides, a sandbox, and a wide field of grass. Troy said the exchange was supposed to happen at two in the afternoon.

Milly parked near the playground and shut off the engine. There were no other cars around. It was 1:30. The park was empty. I thought that was odd. A sunny Saturday afternoon, and no one in the park.

"We'll just wait," Troy said. It was quiet, except for cars buzzing past on the interstate. A kid on a skateboard rolled down the street toward the park. He stepped off his board, kicked it up into his hands, and walked toward the Caddy. Troy waved. The kid stopped a few feet from the car.

"Who the hell are you?" the kid said.

"I'm here to make the exchange," Troy said.

"Where's the regular dude?"

"He was unable to attend."

The kid was shaking his head. "I don't think so. Nope." He dropped the skateboard and stepped on it.

Troy climbed out of the car with the bag. "I've got the stuff, here it is."

"A big Caddy with a bunch of white people inside. Everything about this looks wrong," the kid said. He started to roll away.

"Will you wait a damn minute? Just take the bag."

The kid stopped and grabbed the bag. "Ok, I'll be right back."

"Should I come with you?" Troy said.

"No, you should not come with me. You should get your ass back in the car and wait."

The kid pushed off against the pavement, rolling down the street.

Troy climbed back in the car. "I hope that was the right thing to do?"

I looked at the clock on the dashboard: 2:17. We were still several hours from Utopia. It was hot and humid sitting in the car with the windows down. The sun was bright, and there were only a few clouds; a thin band of smog floated over the city. I tried to remember where Milly's gun was. Had she shoved it under the front seat? Or was it in the glove box?

Troy leaned back against the seat and closed his eyes.

Milly turned on the radio.

"This is a news bulletin from NASA Control," the voice said. "To return safely back to Earth, the Apollo 13 crew will need to use the Lunar Module's engines to orient the spacecraft so that it can safely splash down. Re-entry into the atmosphere requires a manual burn in order to refine the position of the capsule. Apollo 13 is now more than 150,000 nautical miles from Earth, traveling at a velocity of 4,399 feet per second. We are one hour, eighteen minutes, and twenty

seconds away from a midcourse correction."

The astronauts were struggling to get back home, and I was trying to leave. I closed my eyes, and when I opened them again, the clock read 2:39. The kid on the skateboard was rolling toward the Caddy. Behind him was a tall Black man holding Troy's bag. From the way he was walking, he looked upset, arms swinging back and forth. He yelled something at the kid on the skateboard. The kid stopped.

"Let me do the talking," Troy said.

"We have nothing to say to this gentleman," Rue said. "Damn right, you'll do the talking."

The man walked right up to the Caddy, put his hands on the door, and looked in. "Where's Keith?"

"He was unable to make it," Troy said. "I came in his place."

"That is not an acceptable answer. An acceptable answer would be, Keith is dead or in the hospital. Anything else, I don't want to hear it."

"Sorry to disappoint you, sir. He's not in the hospital, and he's not dead. He asked me to come in his place."

The man looked unconvinced. "Who are these folks?"

"I had car trouble, and these people stopped to help."

"That's just about crazy enough to be believable." The man straightened up and looked at the Caddy. "Whose car is this?"

"It's mine," Rue said.

"What year?"

"1963. It's got a 429-cubic-inch V8 with a 4-speed Hydramatic."

The man was walking around the Caddy now, nodding, looking it over. When he came around to Troy's window, he threw the bag on Troy's lap and leaned in. "Ok. I want you to tell Keith that he is at the very top of my shit list. He's Number One. And if he pulls any more foolishness like this, he will see a very unpleasant side of me. Do you understand?"

Troy nodded.

"Excellent. Now get the hell outta my neighborhood."

21

The day before Christmas 1962, my old man and my sister Nancy were standing in a nearly empty parking lot looking at the saddest selection of Christmas trees I'd ever seen. A few weeks earlier, my father had received his new orders. Report immediately to the Yuma Proving Ground. Yuma, Arizona, is about thirty miles from the Mexican border, in the middle of the desert. It's a huge area, thousands of square miles of dry, rocky, uninhabited terrain. Perfect for testing the army's latest weapons. When she heard the news, my Mother asked my father if we could wait until after the holidays to make the move. The army doesn't recognize holidays, he said. So, a week before Christmas, my Mother began calling moving companies, packing boxes, making all the preparations for an unexpected move to the desert, twelve hundred miles away.

"What about Christmas?" Nancy asked.

"Cancelled," my father said.

It was a long, quiet drive from Junction City, Kansas, to Yuma, Arizona. The old man found a cheap motel near the army base, and that was our home for a few weeks until our furniture arrived. My father reported for duty the day before Christmas. My Mother sat in our motel room, sipping wine and scanning the classified ads, looking for a house to rent. When the old man got back from work, Nancy and I jumped to our feet, pleading to get a Christmas tree. He looked around the cramped motel room.

"Where would we put a tree?" he said.

It was dark when we began our search, cruising the empty streets of that dusty little town. Most of the tree lots were closed. Who buys a tree a few hours before Christmas? Finally, we found a small tree lot next to a hardware store. As we pulled up, a man was closing the gate. He'd already turned out the lights.

"We won't be long," my father said.

"Make it quick," the man said. "I got a family dinner."

There wasn't much to choose from; most of the trees had dried out in the desert air. The needles were brown and brittle. Nancy and I ran through the bare lot looking for a small evergreen that would fit in the corner of our motel room. I noticed my old man standing quietly among the trees, looking up. The night sky was incredible in the desert. Millions of bright lights tossed into a black sea. Was he thinking about why he'd dragged his family to this barren little spot at the far edge of the country? Or was he just looking at the stars?

Nancy ran up holding a small, dry spruce. "This one," she said.

The man was standing at the gate when we walked up with our tree.

"That one's twenty-five," he said.

"Twenty-five?" my father said. "You're joking. It's Christmas Eve. In a few hours, it won't be worth anything."

"I'm in a hurry," the man said. "Do you want it or not?"

"I don't want it for twenty-five. Look at it. It's been sitting in the sun for weeks with no water. I'll give you fifteen."

Nancy and I looked away, embarrassed by two grown men haggling over the price of a Christmas tree. The tree man took a deep breath and exhaled. He looked tired, and he wanted to go home.

"Twenty," he said.

"You know how hard I have to work for twenty bucks?" my father said.

"Look, mister," the man said, "in the summer I sell fireworks and cheap jewelry on the side of the road. At Christmas, I sell trees. The tenth of every month, I get a disability check from the Navy. You don't work any harder than I do. Now take the fucking tree and get the hell out of here."

Troy asked if we could drop him off at the bus station. He looked a little down, holding the bag in his lap.

"How much did you get?" I asked.

"I'm not even going to count it," he said. "I know it's not enough."

"Once school is out, maybe you and Ivy can get away for a while," Milly said.

Troy shrugged. "I think about her one way in the morning and something different in the afternoon. I've been a teacher for ten years, and I've just begun to realize that I hate it. The kids are always the same age, and I keep getting older; it's depressing. I don't know if I love Ivy or if I'm just bored with my life."

Milly pulled to a stop in front of the bus station, and Troy climbed out. He waved at Rue and Cora in the backseat, then leaned in the open window.

"Thanks for your help," he said.

"What are you gonna do now?" Milly said.

He smiled. "I'll either turn to a life of crime or get my real estate license. I'm tired of working all day and half the night and coming home with nothing in my pocket."

Milly climbed out of the car with her camera. "We need a picture."

It was weird, the four of us standing in the sun on the sidewalk. Troy put his arm around Rue and Cora, and we all smiled. Milly aimed the camera and pushed the button.

We made it back to the interstate and headed west toward San Antonio. Everyone was quiet for miles, passing through Houston, the sun bright and high in the blue sky. And then Rue spoke up, "No more vagabonds, wandering musicians, gypsies, or dope peddlers. And no more roadside drama. We're going to have a nice, quiet ride all the way to Utopia."

We stopped for gas and Cora, and I changed places. She wanted to sit up front with Milly. They immediately started laughing and talking. I wanted to hear what they were saying, so I leaned forward. They stopped talking, and Cora glared at me. I sat back and leaned against the door, pretending to be asleep, but I could still hear what Milly was saying.

"My first year at school, I lived in a coed dorm," Milly said. "This guy lived across the hall from me, and we were sort of friends. We'd go to movies, grab a pizza once in a while. He was short and his ears stuck out. His name was Carl, but everyone called him Dink. He was funny, very sarcastic, and didn't take anything seriously. His whole focus that semester was on getting laid. He tried with me the first few weeks, and I told him no fucking way, it wasn't going to happen.

"Then he got real serious, asked me how I get a girl into bed? I told him I had no idea. He asked what had worked on me. I had to think about it. I'd only had a few encounters by that time. I thought about sex a lot over the next few days. Why do women go to bed with some men and not others? Physical attraction was part of it, but there had to be something else. Maybe it was a combination of mood, time, and place.

"I knew a girl in high school who slept with this boy because she wanted a ride on his motorcycle. The guy was average-looking and not that smart, but she really wanted a ride on that bike. After a few weeks, she dropped him; the thrill was gone, I guess. For me, it was different. I'd been going with this guy for a few months, we'd done all the preliminaries, but had never gone all the way. One afternoon, we found ourselves in an empty house with a few hours to kill. Sex seemed the next logical step. Was it fun? Sort of. I can't speak for him, but for me, there was very little lust involved. I was more curious about how my body worked, how his body worked. It was more about education than gratification.

"When I saw Dink a few days later, he asked if I had any advice, any insight into how to get laid. I told him every woman was different and there was no formula, no method for convincing her to have sex with you. Women should be approached individually. He nodded. I could almost hear him thinking. That's when he came up with the 99 out of 100 Rule. He said he was going to ask every woman he came into contact with to have sex with him. He predicted that ninetynine out of a hundred would say no. But all I need is one, he said. I thought it was a terrible idea. But what did I know? Maybe hundreds of years of flirtation, romance, and intrigue were all bullshit. Maybe the direct approach was best.

"At first, his scheme seemed a little crude. We'd be standing in line to buy movie tickets, and Dink would turn to the girl behind us and ask her casually if she'd go to bed with him. Sometimes he'd get a slap across the face or a punch in the stomach. Other times, the girl would step back, look him over, and slowly shake her head. Or she would glance at me with a confused look on her face. I'd just shrug my shoulders.
Dink was smart enough not to approach a girl and her boyfriend. The girl had to be alone or in a group of girls. It didn't matter if I was

with him or he was alone; every day was another chance to test his rule.

"It was near the end of the semester. Finals were coming up, and I hadn't seen Dink in a while. Then one afternoon, there he was coming down the hall with a big smile on his face. He told me he'd finally had success with the girl who sat behind him in chemistry class. I asked what she'd said.

"It's 1966, the girl said, there's no valid reason why I'm still a virgin.

"The rule had worked for a few days, and then it didn't. She dumped him. I guess Dink needed another rule for keeping the girl.

"When I saw him during finals, he looked sad and tired, but everyone looked like that during finals. Late one night, I heard a loud bang. I opened my door and looked into the hall. The noise had come from Dink's room. I knocked, but there was no answer. I tried the door, and it was unlocked. Dink was sitting on his bed holding a pistol in his lap. His books were all lined up on his desk, and the end book had a gaping hole in it.

"I wanted to see if a bullet would go all the way through my books," he said.

"The police came, took the gun away, and escorted him to the hospital. He didn't come back the next semester."

22

The sun was down behind the trees when we rolled into Utopia. The soft golden light made everything look peaceful. Rue was sitting up front. Milly was still behind the wheel.

I don't know what I had expected, but Utopia wasn't much. Downtown had a few dozen storefronts, a courthouse in the middle of town, a water tower, and a single traffic light.

"Our shoe store used to be in that building across from the courthouse," Rue said. "Until it burned down." "What happened?" I asked.

"The phone rang late one night, and Calvin picked it up," Rue said. "It was our neighbor telling us a group of angry white folks was gathering downtown, setting fire to the courthouse. A few days prior, I'd read in the paper that a Negro man, named George Hughes, had been arrested for assaulting a white woman and had been taken to the jail under the courthouse. This was a lynch mob looking for his blood. Calvin hung up the phone and began to dress. I'll get the shotgun, I said. He told me there was no way I was going down there with him. I told him I was going if I had to walk. "When we arrived, the courthouse was in flames. The blaze was so hot we had to cover our faces with our coats. The fire department had given up and was standing across the street, watching. Two Texas Rangers with shotguns were trying to keep the crowd under control. It was a futile effort. A large mob filled the streets, cheering, shouting awful things. We watched, speechless as the flames grew in size until the blaze reached across the street and set fire to several buildings. Calvin dragged hoses from the back room and began to spray the front of our store with water. The mob began to move away from the courthouse and up the street. A single enraged mass, looking for more Black victims. I stood in the doorway of our store holding the shotgun. I have never seen such ugly, hateful faces. Men and women, folks I knew. There were children in that vicious mob, pulled along by their parents, sitting on their Daddy's shoulders like this was a street carnival. It disgusted me.

"Secretly, I hoped someone in the crowd would try to loot our store, giving me an excuse to use the shotgun. But no one approached. The roaring mob moved off, the courthouse burned to the ground, and the Black man was consumed in the fire. The next day, I read in the paper that the crowd attacked the Black business district, north of the courthouse, and burned down all the shops. Most of the Black folks in town packed up their belongings and drove away in the middle of the night. And never returned.

The only place in Utopia that looked busy was a large wooden building on the edge of town. Cars and trucks

filled up the lawn out front. Above the open barn doors was a sign:
Hadley Dance Hall.

"What's that?" I said.

"It's a dance hall," Rue said.

"What's a dance hall?"

"It's where folks go to drink and dance and get in trouble."

"We should stop," Cora said, "looks like fun."

"Take me to the boarding house," Rue said, "then you all can get in all the trouble you want."

Rue directed Milly through town down a winding ranch road. There were wire fences on both sides, and cattle grazing in the fields. A river ran alongside the road. We came to a long gravel driveway that led to a large two-story house surrounded by trees. The house was dark.

Milly parked, Rue climbed out, walked to the front door, and rang the bell. A light went on, and Rue spoke to the woman who answered the door, then walked back to the car.

"We're like family now," Rue said, sarcastically. She handed Cora a key. "Jim and I are in one room, you and Milly in the other."

The dance hall was a big white barn that had been converted into a bar. Through the wide doors, we could see tables and chairs and a large dance floor. A band was playing on a stage at the far end of the hall. The place was jammed with people, dancing and drinking. Milly, Cora, and I stood against a wall watching the crowd. An older man walked past and touched the brim of his cowboy hat.

I had managed to go the entire day without much to eat. I tried to remember my last meal: a bag of potato chips and a Dr. Pepper when we stopped for gas in Houston. Cora and Milly walked to the bar, and I wandered outside to a large cement patio with wooden tables. Christmas lights were strung from the roof of the dance hall to the trees and around the patio. A man stood behind a barbecue pit, sweet smoke pouring from the pit. The patio was full of people sitting at tables, drinking beer, and eating off paper plates. A young couple was doing slow turns across the cement floor. I ordered a brisket plate and looked around for an empty seat, but all the tables were full. A man in a cowboy hat stood up and waved, "Hey, boy. Come sit with us."

I took a seat and shook hands with him. Everyone at the table looked drunk, glassy-eyed, and hunched over their beers.

"What's your name, son?" The man said.

I told him my name and said I was in town for a funeral.

"Have a beer," he said.

He took a bottle from a bucket of ice, opened it, and set it in front of me. The woman sitting next to him leaned closer and said, "If you're just gonna sit here all night and get drunk, I'm gonna find someone to dance with."

"Be my guest, sweetheart," the man said. He lifted his hat and waved it at her as she walked away. Then he put his arm around me. "Best two thousand dollars I ever spent."

"Excuse me?"

"They ask you when you walk in the door, do you prefer oranges or melons? I said melons, right away. I'm paying for 'em, so I wanted something I can catch hold of, gimme some purchase. Know what I mean?"

"I'm not sure what you're talking about."

"Tits, jugs, boobies…everybody's got a favorite size. I like 'em big."

I nodded, not sure what to say.

"When she comes back, check out her rack. But don't let her catch you doing it or she'll slap the shit out of you."

His name was Earl Tatum, and he worked in the oil equipment business. Two days a month, he was a volunteer fireman in Utopia.

"Your trailer fire is the worst," Earl said. He was leaning on me, slurring his words. "There's no saving 'em once they get going. Just cheap plywood and plastic. And they burn hot."

He took a long drink of beer.

"We got a call last year, late in the day. When we rolled up, flames were shooting out the sides of the trailer, and there was this woman standing in the street, screaming her head off. 'My boy's inside.' I looked at the trailer and thought to myself, if he's in there, he's a goner. My buddy grabs the woman and pulls her back from the flames, and we start throwing water over the trailer. There was no saving it, but we needed to keep the fire contained. I'm standing there with a firehose pushing water as fast as it will travel, and bullets start going off. Bang, bang, bang. I'm thinking, who in the hell is shooting at us? I hit the deck and cover my head. Shooting goes on for some time. Turns out it was ammunition in the trailer, going off.

"The cops roll up about this time and get control of the woman. She's sitting on the curb with her head in her hands, drunk. She'd gone next door to have a few cold ones with her neighbor, left her four-year-old by himself. The boy musta found some matches and set fire to the trailer. It was awful. The woman collapsed on the curb, crying, carrying on. Cops didn't know what to do. We didn't know what to do. Then I look up and see this older woman walking toward us, holding this kid's hand. It's her boy. He'd set fire to the trailer, then had enough sense to run away."

Earl took a drink. "Some folks can't have kids, and then there's this woman who doesn't know how to raise the one she got."

I sat there for hours talking to Earl and his friends. There were dozens of empty bottles on the table when they stood up and said goodbye. They were all drunk, holding on to each other.

Earl stopped and looked back at me.

"You know what they say in Texas, boy?" Earl said, gesturing toward the empty beer bottles.

I shook my head.

"I'd rather have a bottle in front of me than a frontal lobotomy."

He started laughing, staggering toward the parking lot.

I stood up and had to put a hand on the table to steady myself. I didn't realize how drunk I was. As soon as I stepped inside the hall, the band stopped playing, put down their instruments, and went outside for a cigarette. I stood by the open barn doors, looking for Cora and Milly. The crowd began to drift outside to get some air and to smoke. It was quiet, warm, and still, crickets singing in the shadows.

The band's drummer was talking to a young cowboy and his girlfriend. The cowboy started shaking his finger at the drummer. Their voices got louder, a few harsh words were exchanged, and then punches were thrown. A crowd gathered around the two men rolling around on the grass. The drummer landed a solid punch on the cowboy's face. The girlfriend knelt down to help the cowboy to his feet.

"I quit her," the drummer shouted, "she's yours."

The cowboy picked up his hat and walked away with his girlfriend. The drummer looked at his hand. One of his fingers was bent at an unnatural angle. The guitar player walked over to have a look.

"Well, I guess that's it for tonight. Can't play with a busted finger."

A man pushed through the crowd and confronted the guitar player. "You owe me another set," he said. "Now get your ass back on that stage, or you can forget about your money."

The guitar player nodded, then walked slowly over to his truck, opened his guitar case, and took something out. The crowd saw the gun in his hand and stepped back.

"I want my money, you fucking hillbilly," the guitar player said, the gun loose at his side. The man reached into his jeans, pulled out a stack of bills, and threw them at the guitar player.

The excitement was over, and people started drifting slowly back to their cars. I walked to the Caddy and tried the doors, which were locked. I crawled on the hood and leaned back against the windshield. I thought about walking back to the boardinghouse, but I wasn't sure I could find it in the dark. I must have fallen asleep because when I opened my eyes, the dance hall was dark and the parking lot was nearly empty. Milly and Cora were walking across the parking lot. Milly was smoking a cigarette.

I jumped down from the car. "I couldn't find you. Where were you?"

"You're not my Mother, Jim," Milly said.

I stepped close, trying to give her a hug. "You're so pretty," I said.

She pushed me away.

"You're drunk," Cora said.

Milly took a drag on the cigarette and blew smoke at me. "Pretty used to mean a lot, it doesn't anymore. Now I want to be competent."

Cora and Milly leaned against the Caddy, passing the cigarette back and forth.

"I was raised to believe in a good God, a bad Devil, and a hot hell," Cora said. "You were going straight to the eternal fires if you had sex before you got married. All that seems like bullshit now."

"Always was bullshit," Milly said. "Men use religion to control women. Can't have the ladies enjoying themselves."

Cora put her arm around Milly. They were both smiling, their faces red.

"The golden age of sex has arrived," Cora said. "We've got the pill so we won't get knocked up, penicillin in case of the clap…and there are a whole lot of women out there ready for some good old-fashioned, no-strings-attached fucking."

23

I had a job as an usher in a movie theater for a while. I wore this dumb red vest and carried a flashlight to help people find a seat. After the movie, I had to clean up all the popcorn and candy. The floor was always a sticky mess from spilled soda. I hated that part of the job, but I loved watching movies. I'd sit in the back row when the manager was gone and watch the same movie over and over. I could see the same movie ten times and, because the crowd was different each time, I always saw something I hadn't seen before. Movies let me escape the everyday bullshit of my stupid life. Sitting in the dark with hundreds of strangers, all feeling the same emotions at the same time. Something amazing was happening up on the screen, bigger than life. It was impossible to look away.

Early the next morning, someone was shaking my arm. It was Rue. "The service is in two hours. Get dressed and meet me downstairs."

I'd packed a dark gray suit for the funeral. My Mother bought it for me years ago when we were still going to church. When I tried on the pants, the legs were several inches above my ankles. The shirt was tight across my shoulders, and the collar wouldn't button. I put the coat over my arm and walked downstairs. Cora, Milly, and Rue were sitting at a long table eating breakfast.

Rue shook her head when she saw me. "There's no time to get you something that fits. Just don't tell anyone your name is Birdwell."

"You look like a waiter who got caught in the rain," Cora said.

"I don't know why I'm going," Milly said, "I didn't even know Uncle Percy."

"It's about respect," Rue said. "You've come this far, don't you want to see how it ends?"

"It always ends the same," Milly said, "a big hole in the ground, a casket, people crying."

The service was being held at the First Baptist Church, a small church just off the main street in Utopia. When Milly parked out front, there were only a few cars in the parking lot. It was Sunday, the Baptist service was over, and the place was empty. When we stepped inside, a woman was vacuuming the carpet. She looked up and turned it off. "You all here for the memorial service?"

We took a seat in the front pew. A polished wooden casket rested on a table next to the altar. The church was quiet. Through the windows, I could see clouds moving across the sky.

We've traveled twelve hundred miles to be here, I thought. I hope someone shows up.

I looked at Rue. She seemed calm. I took her hand, and she smiled at me. "Thanks for bringing me home, Jim."

I turned around to see an older man entering the church and, a few steps behind him, a younger man about my age. The older man walked to the front of the church, turned, and smiled at Rue. "That ain't fair, Rue. I get older every year, and you stay the same."

Rue stood up, walked over, and hugged the man. "Matty, you shouldn't be telling lies in church." She was smiling, holding his hands.

"This is my old friend, Mateo Santos," she said. "I don't know who this young fellow is."

"This is Gabby, my grandson," Matty said.

Mateo kissed Rue on the cheek, and they took a seat behind us.

A tall man wearing a gray fedora and a long black coat entered the church. He was escorting a younger woman. The woman was Percy's second wife, Lena. I'd seen pictures of her. They found seats near the front of the church and sat down. It was quiet again.

After a few minutes, the preacher walked up the center aisle, stepped behind the altar, and looked out over the nearly empty pews. "I guess we should get started."

He opened a Bible and began to read. I don't remember any of it. My head was still foggy from the night before. I just remember how quiet the church was until Rue leaned toward me and whispered, "Percy didn't believe in all this stuff."

The preacher read a few more passages from the Bible and said a long prayer. The woman who'd been vacuuming appeared at the organ and began to play. That was our cue to leave.

We all filed out of the church and stood outside in the shade. Lena introduced the tall man in the fedora as Frederic Meyer, Percy's brother-in-law. He removed his hat and took Rue's hand. "I am so glad to finally meet you. We have much to talk about. Perhaps we can have dinner before you leave?"

Rue looked stunned, unable to speak. I'm not sure she knew Frederic even existed. He stood there smiling at her, erasing the years, a direct connection to her brother Percy.

We all turned to watch the man from the funeral home wheeling the casket down the sidewalk to the hearse waiting at the curb. My brain wasn't fully awake. I felt like when I open my eyes in the morning after a long, deep sleep. That unreal, in-between state. Not fully awake and not asleep. This dazed feeling ended abruptly when the man from the funeral home slammed the hearse door shut and drove off.

The Utopia Cemetery was located on a hill a few miles from town. A rusty iron fence surrounded the small graveyard. Clumps of dry grass and wildflowers grew in the dirt between the headstones. I wandered among the graves, reading the inscriptions:

Eddy Morrow was shot by a deputy on July 12, 1903.

Mary Reed died in May 1918, taken by the Spanish Flu.

Alma Childress. Died in 1923.

Harvey Childress. Died in 1927.

Calvin Birdwell. Died in 1951.

Next to the family headstones was a deep hole in the rocky ground.

Rue found a grassy spot in the shade and sat down. She had on a wide black hat as big as a dinner plate. She took it off and laid it in the grass. We all sat down next to her. I'd never seen Milly in a dress. When she folded her legs under her, I noticed a small tattoo on her ankle: a red heart with a knife through it.

"You never told us what happened to Calvin," Milly said.

"Calvin." Rue shook her head. "The man was born in the wrong century. The things he believed to be true just didn't fit the times he lived in. And we didn't have much in common. But in the end, most folks are adaptable. Once two people have learned each other's peculiarities and understand their family dramas, a marriage usually settles down. Ours did. We only had the one child, which seemed like enough. Once the Depression was through with us, things began to go our way. Turns out, people always need shoes.

"When Robert came along, Calvin had this absurd idea that military school would be good for the boy. Calvin somehow had missed out on both wars, but wanted his son to be a soldier. I tried my best to stop it, but Calvin put his foot down and sent the boy away when he was twelve. The last thing a twelve-year-old boy needs is military training. He needs his family, his friends. A boy needs to be outdoors climbing trees, not marching around holding a gun."

Rue took my hand. "Jim, your father is the way he is because of that school. The damage was done and cannot be undone. Calvin always wanted to be right, and he wanted me to admit I was wrong. I couldn't do it, and he resented me for it. So, we settled into an uneasy routine. Routines can be dangerous things. Given time, folks can adapt to anything. Old habits keep you from new thinking, keep you from changing. I stayed married to Calvin because I didn't see any other way. Back then, women didn't have choices; they had roles, not like today, not like you two ladies.

"Calvin always had a problem with food, couldn't tolerate spicy dishes. No salt, no pepper, no hot sauce. His favorite dinner was macaroni and cheese with a glass of milk. He never gained weight or lost it. Stayed a constant one hundred forty-five pounds. Wore the same brown suit and gray fedora, Monday through Saturday. On Sundays, he switched to the blue pinstripe with a red tie. He was a solid yellow-dog Democrat all his life, a faithful member of the Kiwanis Club, and a generous contributor to the Lutheran Church. He was honest, reliable, and straightforward. He woke up one morning complaining of a pain in his stomach. Said he'd had it for months. I nagged him to go see a doctor, which he did reluctantly. He told me the doctor said it was an ulcer. I found out later that it was stomach cancer. The doctor told Calvin he had less than a year. My husband kept the news to himself and went about his business like nothing was wrong.

"We had a nice two-story home in Utopia with a big garden, lots of trees. One afternoon, Calvin came home for lunch, something he often did. I fixed him a ham and cheese sandwich and poured him a glass of milk, then I went out in the garden. It was early spring, and I wanted to start some seeds in one of the beds. I was kneeling down with my hands in the dirt when I heard a soft bang. I thought it was a car backfiring. I walked into the kitchen. Calvin wasn't there, but his car was still in the driveway. I called out his name, walking through the house. No answer. I went upstairs and saw the attic ladder pulled down. What was he doing in the attic? I climbed the ladder and saw him lying there. The gun was still in his hand."

We were all quiet, sitting in the grass. The day had begun to warm up. Green hills in the distance. Thick clouds, like white roaming mountains, are floating across the blue sky. Milly moved closer to Rue, reached out, and held her hand.

When I saw the black hearse coming down the long road to the cemetery, I stood up and helped Rue to her feet.

Frederic, Matty, Gabby, and I carried the casket from the hearse to the grave. Our small group gathered around the hole in the ground, waiting for the preacher. I looked at Lena. She must have been much younger than Uncle

Percy. Percy was in his seventies when he died, but his widow didn't look that old. Her face was blank, head down, holding on to
Frederic's arm.

The preacher drove up, climbed out of his car, and walked over to our small group. "What a beautiful day," he said, opening his Bible. He began to read from Psalms, something about green pastures and still waters. A loud noise interrupted the reading, a sound like rushing water. The preacher closed the Bible and looked around. "What is that?"

At first, I thought it was a bird or a squirrel. I glanced up into the trees, but the noise seemed to be coming from under my feet. And it was getting louder. Matty stepped forward and looked down into the open grave. "There's a rattlesnake down there."

Everyone moved closer for a better look. Coiled in one corner, its head curved up from its body, was a huge snake.

Matty turned and walked to his truck. No one moved. No one said a word. He came back holding a pistol. "Everyone step back, please."

He pointed the gun down into the hole and pulled the trigger. The angry hissing stopped. Matty stuck the pistol in his belt. The preacher opened his Bible. "Now where was I?"

Rue leaned close and whispered, "Percy would have loved that."

24

Frederic invited everyone to lunch at a Mexican restaurant in town. He'd arranged a private room for family and friends. Well, not a private room exactly. Three tables pushed together out on a stone patio. When Rue stepped out on the patio, Frederic pulled back a chair and motioned for her to sit. He shook hands with everyone, introducing himself, asking the waitress to bring drinks and appetizers. Margaritas, beer, chips and salsa, guacamole, and queso soon filled the tables.

The funeral had done a number on my head. I was happy it wasn't me in that casket, and I felt good about myself for getting Rue safely to the funeral, but at the same time, I was panicked about the draft letter and what to do about it. I was a long way from home, and I wasn't sure I was ever going back. Rue's stories about her past made her life seem like a series of violent, random accidents. And Milly's story wasn't much better. I only knew a few things for certain. I didn't want to go to Vietnam, I didn't want to run away to Mexico or Canada, and I wanted to sleep with Milly.
It didn't seem possible for all those things to happen.

I sat on one side of Rue, Frederic on the other. Cora and Gabby leaned close to each other, smiling, talking.

Lena, Milly, and Matty were at the other end of the table, all smiling. Matty was telling a story, waving his hands around, maybe he was reenacting the death of the snake.

Frederic asked Rue the last time she'd seen her brother. She told him the story of taking the bus out to California a few years earlier, meeting Lena, and going to the beach.

"I miss my brother," she said. "Meeting you makes me miss him even more."

Frederic reached into his pocket for an envelope. Inside the envelope was a faded black-and-white photo, frayed at the edges. He handed it to Rue. "The only picture I have of my family."

"Oh my God. I have the same one. It's Percy's wedding."

"June, 1928," Frederic said, "Treptower Park, Berlin. It was a beautiful day. After the wedding at the temple, we all went to a restaurant and got very drunk on champagne and cognac. Marta was very happy. My Mother…not so thrilled. Her only daughter is marrying a gentile and an American."

"My Mother wasn't very happy either," Rue said.

Frederic took a postcard out of his pocket and began to read:

We are waiting for the trains that will take us to the work camps. Our departure was scheduled several days ago, but has been postponed again. Mother and Father have aged many years in the past few months. First, the indignity of losing the restaurant, and now the humiliation of being confined to our apartment. But not to worry. Percy goes to the American Embassy every morning to try to obtain immigration visas. He says it is only a formality. We are hopeful he will be successful. I pray every morning, knowing that God will not abandon us. Will write again soon when I have more news.

Love and hugs, Marta.

"How did you escape?" I said.

Frederic looked at me.

"I was sent to Paris by my father as a young man to learn the banking business. Thankfully, numbers have remained a mystery to me all my life. I was more interested in art, music, and women. I bought three small drawings by Chagall. He was living in Paris then. I knew him for a brief time. He gave me a deal, as he was short on cash. Soon after, I traded those drawings for a very early Degas, which I then reluctantly sold to an American businessman. I made a sizable amount of money on the sale, but I still miss that painting."

He paused and seemed to be lost in his thoughts, then said, "What were we talking about?"

"Oh, yes. My escape from Europe. I was in Paris when the Nuremberg Laws were passed. Gesetz zum Schutze des Deutschen Blutes und der Deutschen Ehre. Which means: For the protection of German blood and German honor. The new laws divided Jewish people into optimists and pessimists. I was a pessimist. I wrote my father, begging them to come to Paris. Our country does not want us anymore; it will only get worse, and this is just the beginning. My father wrote back that our family has been in Germany for centuries.

The Nazis are a temporary political fashion, he said, they will be voted out soon enough.

"My father was an optimist; he believed the momentum of history moves toward equality and justice. The twentieth century is proving him wrong."

Rue took Frederic's hand. "You don't have to talk about this."

"No, it's fine. My therapist is always telling me I must confront these memories."

Frederic looked up at the green hills, the clouds rolling by overhead. "I've never been to Texas. I imagined many cows, horses…cactus."

"We have all that," Rue said. "And flowers. Lots of wildflowers."

"I like how you can look out over the land and see for miles, no buildings, no people."

The waitress walked past, and Frederic ordered shots of tequila for everyone. She disappeared inside and returned with a tray, setting a shot glass in front of everyone at the table. Frederic stood up, raised his glass, and said, "To Percy." And threw back the tequila. We all did the same.

Frederic sat back down. "The rest of my story is not so traumatic. Once the Germans occupied Paris, the French government declared Jews to be enemy aliens.

Time to go. I took a train south as far as Toulouse, and then I walked. It was a beautiful summer. I slept in barns and under trees. And then one morning, I strolled over the mountains into Spain. I thought about staying in Madrid, but who knew what these Germans were capable of. They wanted the whole world. At least America was an ocean away. So, I took a steamer to New York and enrolled in City College to study business. I became an American. No time for Paris and art and all that old-world foolishness. I married a very funny woman. She passed away several years ago. I still miss her jokes. We had no children. We both thought it reckless to bring a child into this world. I went into the insurance business." He shrugged. "Yes, I know, how boring."

Frederic put his hand on Rue's arm and leaned close. "Tell me about yourself."

I looked at the two of them. They'd once been family, now they were trying to make the years disappear. It was time to leave them alone. I walked to the end of the table and sat down next to Milly and Lena. They were both smiling, faces red. Milly was talking to Lena, and she sounded a little drunk.

"Every boyfriend is like a new religion," Milly was saying. "New stories to learn, new ways to do everything. Shutting off part of my brain so he'll think he's smarter than me."

She took a drink of beer. "I was living in Austin. Sleeping in parks, under bridges. I was cold and miserable. I woke up in the middle of the night, shivering, and my head felt like someone was pounding on it. I walked to a coffee shop, trying to warm up. I must have passed out because when I woke up, I was in this guy's car.

"'I'm taking you to the hospital,' he says.

"He carries me inside, they stick tubes in my arm, and give me something to knock me out. It was pneumonia. A few days later, I'm released from the hospital, and he's waiting for me. He introduces himself. Curtis Dupree. Says he's taking me to his place.

"'You need rest and antibiotics,' he said. 'Don't worry. I'm not a weirdo. I just don't want you to die in the park.'

"He had a nice house, a huge yard, big trees. I had my own room. He gave me money to buy clothes. He seemed lonely. I guess we both needed someone. He told me he couldn't trust anyone because of the business he was in. He sold weed at the university, had a whole crew of student dealers.

"We started sleeping together, and I got involved in his business. Every week, he'd dump a load of cash on the dining room table, and I'd count it. I convinced him to invest in stocks and real estate. He was making a lot of money, but it wasn't enough. Thought he could make a lot more if he started selling Coke. I told him the kids who were buying weed were not the same people who bought coke. Coke is expensive; you need a job to afford it. All Curtis could see was the money. I asked him how much money would be enough. I asked him if he wanted to still be dealing when he was thirty or forty. He laughed at me.

A year ago, you were sleeping under a bridge, he said, now you're telling me to run my fucking business.

"Then things started to get weird. He'd come home late at night or early in the morning, coked up and ready to get it on. But Coke is not the best drug for late-night sex. Most nights, he couldn't get it up, which made him really mad. We stopped having sex, and since we weren't fucking, he assumed I was doing it with someone else. He got really paranoid and started having me followed. I began to feel like a prisoner.

"One night, he came home completely coked out of his mind. He grabbed me around the neck, threw me down, and tried to rape me. But his equipment wouldn't work. He gave up and passed out. It was early morning, so I went to the kitchen, made coffee, and put my sneakers in the dryer. I was sitting in the kitchen trying to figure out how to get away from this psycho when the dog started whining. I go to see about the dog, and Curtis is standing in the hall with a gun. I ask him what the hell's going on, and he tells me to shut up. He's moving slowly toward the laundry room, pistol up, ready. My shoes are going round and round in the dryer, making a big noise. I try to tell him it's just my sneakers, but he won't let me talk. He kicks the laundry room door open and puts three bullet holes in the dryer. The dryer didn't stop turning. That was a damn good dryer.

"I knew I had to leave, but I didn't have enough money, so I started putting a little aside every week. After a few months, I had seven hundred bucks stashed. One afternoon, I put the money in my bag and headed for the grocery store just like always. The guy he hired to follow me doesn't even bother to go inside with me. So, I walk in the front door and out the back, catch a taxi, and by the time he's missing me, I'm at the bus station. I climb on the bus, and I'm heading to Florida.

"After a few hours, I start to lose my nerve, start to panic. I notice this young guy sitting across the aisle. He's about my age, so I go over and sit next to him. The look on my face must have scared the shit out of him because he asked if I was ok. He asked where I was going, and I showed him my ticket to Florida.

You don't want to go there, he said, come to New Orleans with me.

"I leaned against his shoulder and slept all the way to New Orleans. We found a cheap hotel with a balcony overlooking the street. After a long, hot shower, I climbed into bed, exhausted, anxious, scared. I was all alone, except for this stranger. My money would soon be gone, and what the hell would I do then? But the bed was soft, the sheets were clean, and my new friend was in the shower, singing a Beatles song. His voice sounded so sweet. Over the bed was a cross with a plaster Jesus. Sounds from the street floated up into the room, and when the kid came out of the shower, I gave him a blowjob, and we fell asleep.

Milly looked at Lena and asked if she knew what a blowjob was.

Lena smiled. "You young people think you invented sex. There is nothing new in the bedroom, child. It's just new to you."

25

It was late in the afternoon when I got to my room and collapsed on the bed. I don't know who drove us back to the boarding house. Rue, I guess. She was the least drunk person at the table.

I lay on the bed staring at the ceiling fan, the room spinning slowly, thinking about my life. I'd only been alive eighteen years, and with so little to remember, I should have been able to recall a coherent string of events from my childhood. A collection of memories that had led me to where I was now. That wasn't the case. Maybe it was the result of moving around so often. My memory is a disjointed series of episodes, connected only by the fact that I experienced them. One incident does not lead to the next in any orderly progression.

I remember falling when I was small, cutting my wrist on a piece of glass, the blood pulsing from the wound. And the shocked look on my Mother's face.

And years later, another memory fragment. I'm chasing my sister through a pasture at night, and I run into the barbed wire fence. The wire slices my forehead just above my eyes. My father picks me up and drives me to the hospital. I remember the stunned expression on his face. Was he annoyed or concerned? Another image from the past. My father is driving through Arizona. I'm standing up in the front seat. A truck had broken down on the side of the road, and my father stopped to help. The driver did not speak English, and my father didn't know Spanish. I stood in the sun, on the side of the road, while the two men looked at the engine, gesturing to each other. Finally, my father attached a rope to the truck and pulled it to a service station. I remember the man tried to pay my father for his help. My father would not take his money, so the man went inside and came back with a Coke and a candy bar and handed them to me. The two men shook hands, and we drove off.

I woke up in the night, and the room was empty. I walked downstairs and stepped outside. Milly and Cora were sitting on the porch, smoking.

"Where's Rue?"

"Out with her new boyfriend."

"We're going wild pig hunting tomorrow," Cora said. "Matty and Gabby invited us. Are you coming?" "I've never held a gun in my life," I said.

"That's ok," Milly smiled. "We'll use you as bait."

It was late afternoon, the day after the funeral. We cruised down a dirt road a few miles west of Utopia. Milly was driving, Cora riding shotgun. Up ahead, Matty and Gabby are in an old rusty Chevy pickup. According to Matty, the few hours before sunset are the best time to hunt wild pigs.

The truck rolled through a dry, rocky landscape of open fields and cedar trees, with a few low hills in the distance. We drove for miles down a rutted, dirt road, the Caddy bouncing over the rough surface. The truck came to a stop, and Milly pulled in behind it. We all climbed out of the Caddy and walked over. Gabby was taking rifles from the truck and handing them to his grandfather.

Matty looked up, "Which of you knows how to handle a weapon?"

Milly and Cora raised their hands.

"Ok," he said, "you ladies go with Gabby. You come with me, chico."

Matty put the rifle across his shoulder and walked toward the trees. I was right behind him. The narrow trail meandered through grassy meadows thick with wildflowers and cactus. Matty was quiet, walking slowly, at times stopping to listen.

"Where did these pigs come from?"

Matty turned to look at me. "They came with the
Spanish…long time ago."

"Do we need a license?"

"Not so loud. Pigs have excellent

hearing." I nodded.

"You don't need a license," he whispered. "Open season, year-round."

We moved off along the trail and came to a wide meadow. The ground was covered with blue flowers.

"Wow," I said, "what are these?"

"Be quiet. Those are bluebonnets."

We walked through the flowers until we came to a dry creek with a sandy bottom. Matty pointed to the ground. "See where the sand has been churned up? Pigs like to roll around in it."

He opened his bag and handed me a pistol. "I want you to stay right here. I'll go around this little hill, see if I can push 'em down the trail."

"Then what?"

"Well…if you see a pig coming down this trail, shoot him." He put a hand on my shoulder. "Just don't shoot me, tu sabes?"

"I've never shot anything before…"

He smiled. "You'll be fine. Just keep your eyes and ears open."

Matty turned and walked into the trees. I sat down in the sand and set the pistol beside me. It's quiet, except for the sound of crickets and birds moving around in the bushes. The sky was slowly fading from a deep blue to a vivid purple.

Sometimes I miss subtle signals from people. A look or a glance. A nod of the head. A tone of voice that goes right past me. Maybe it's because I spend a lot of time in my head and less time in the present. I am trying to change that. I want to participate more in my own life and contemplate less. I was determined to sit there and watch and listen until a pig came down the trail. No daydreaming, no head in the clouds.

After several minutes, the bugs found me. Mosquitoes, gnats, flies, ants. I grabbed the gun and stood up, waving at the swarm of bugs around my head.

A few more minutes and I'll need a flashlight to see anything. Where is Matty?

Then I heard something moving in the shadows just off the trail. It sounded too small to be a pig. Matty said some of the pigs were close to three hundred pounds.

The noise stopped. It was quiet for a few minutes, and then I heard the sound of heavy breathing and soft thuds on the dirt path. Something was running. I looked up the dark trail, the pistol ready.

"Here they come, boy."

A small herd of pigs, nearly invisible in the dark undergrowth, rushed toward me, heads down, grunting softly. The animals were packed tightly together, charging down the trail. In the shadows, they looked like one enormous pig. I waited until they were almost on top of me, raised the pistol, closed my eyes, and pulled the trigger. Over and over, until the gun was empty. The pigs didn't seem to notice me. They passed quickly, disappearing down the trail.

Smoke rose from the barrel, the pistol hot in my hand.

Matty walked out of the dark trees.

"I think I hit something, but I can't be sure."

"Let's go find out."

We walked along the trail, heads down, looking for blood. Up ahead in the shadows, we heard the pigs crashing through the brush. Matty stopped and knelt down. There were drops of blood in the dirt. He put his fingers in the blood and held it in front of my face. "You hit something."

The blood reeks, sharp and bitter, like nothing I have ever smelled before.

"What do we do?"

"We have to find the pig and kill it."

"Won't it just die on its own?"

"It might. But you don't walk away from a wounded animal. It's not right."

I handed the pistol to Matty, he reloaded it, and handed it back. The light was fading fast. It's dark under the trees and in the deep brush. Matty took a flashlight out of his bag, flipped it on, and pointed the beam down the trail. "Vamanos."

We moved quietly along the trail, looking for signs of blood. We crossed fields of dry grass, through dense bushes with thorns that grabbed at our clothes. The trail seemed to be taking us uphill; the trees were sparse, scattered across a rocky ledge. The trail was a thin path in the dirt. We stopped, and Matty knelt down, pointing to a small pool of blood.

"He's bleeding."

We kept moving up along the edge of the ridge until we were beyond the trees. The space above our heads opened into an immense field of stars sweeping across the dark sky.

I stopped and looked up. "Look at the stars."

"Yes, so many. They are always up there. We can only see them when the sun goes away."

Matty directed the light out across the top of the barren hill. The wounded animal was slowly crossing the rocky ground, moving down the far side of the slope.

"Where is the rest of the herd?"

"He's dying. They don't want to be near him."

The wounded pig moved down off the ridge and disappeared into the trees. We followed the trail, thick shrubs crowding the path.

Matty turned to look at me, "Be alert."

I looked down at the gun in my hand. My heart is beating fast.

Matty stopped and pointed the flashlight into a dense thicket. We could see the wounded pig standing deep in the brush, panting, its red eyes reflecting the beam of light.

"You need to go in there and finish him," Matty said.

He handed me the flashlight. The last thing I wanted to do was go in there after a wounded pig. But I didn't want to disappoint Matty. I raised the pistol and took a step into the thicket, vines snagging my shirt and jeans. I moved slowly, the gun in one hand, the light in the other. Moving cautiously, I pulled back the thorns and vines. The pig was backing up now, moving deeper into the undergrowth, making strange sounds, growling, gasping. And then it was quiet. The pig began pawing at the dirt, then suddenly charged forward. I leveled the gun at the pig's head and pulled the trigger three times. The animal slammed into me, knocking me to the ground, and kept going.

I'm breathing heavy now, and my knee hurts. We followed the wounded pig back up the trail and found it lying on its side. The animal's enormous chest is moving up and down. I stepped close, put the barrel of the gun a few feet from the pig's head, and squeezed the trigger. I thought I'd be disgusted, killing an animal, but I wasn't. I didn't feel much of anything.

Matty knelt in the dirt, dipped a finger in the warm blood, and brushed it across my forehead.

"What's that for?"

"This animal gave up its life. You must show your respect."

26

I opened my eyes and sat up in bed. Rue was dressed, standing at the window. A bright moon lit up the room.

"Are you ok?" I said.

"Put your clothes on. We're going somewhere."

"What time is it?"

"Doesn't matter. Just get dressed."

I dressed quickly, followed her down the stairs, and out to the Cadillac. She handed me the keys. "We're going to the cemetery."

"What's going on?"

"You ask a lot of questions. Do what I tell you, boy."

I drove up the gravel drive to the highway. In the moonlight, the river was a silver road curving through the dark trees. Rue was quiet. She opened her purse and dug out something.

I wheeled the Caddy into the cemetery parking lot and turned off the engine.

"I'm going to New York with Frederic," she said. "He's asked me to stay with him for a while. Don't know

how long I'll be up there, and I wanted you to have this."
She opened her hand and held out a coin.

I picked it up and looked at it in the dashboard light.
"What is it?"

"It's called a Caballito, the little horse. One side is the
Mexican coat of arms, an eagle with a snake in its beak.
The other side is a woman riding a horse, holding a torch.
They were minted for only a short time in the early years
of this century. Ninety percent silver."

She took my hand. "Eventually, your father will drive
you out of his house with all his damn rules. My advice is
to take the Caddy and see the country. And take Milly
with you, she'll keep you safe."

"I've been drafted, Rue."

"I know, Milly told me." She pulled me into a hug.
"You don't have to go over there, Jim." She was crying,
her breathing slow, uneven. She held me for some time,
and for those few quiet minutes, everything seemed like
it would work out. And then she let me go and wiped her
face. "There's something else. Come on."

We climbed out of the car. She popped open the
trunk, reached in, and handed me a shovel. We walked
through the quiet graveyard, the moonlight reflecting on
the slabs of marble. She stepped behind Calvin's
headstone and pointed at the ground. "Dig here."

The dry ground was hard and rocky. It took some
effort to loosen the dry, packed soil. I had to pry out
several large rocks. Every time I asked her what was down
there, she smiled and said, "Keep digging."

To pass the time, I asked about her father.

"He was a cotton farmer," she said. "And he hated it. He loved horses, but there wasn't any money in horseflesh until the Spanish-American War came along. The army was looking for mounts to ship to Cuba. My father decided he was going to buy cheap land out West and raise a herd. He told Mother the war would last for years because this country can't resist a good fight. Mother was pregnant with Percy and pleaded with him not to leave her alone. He ignored her and bought some land in West Texas and built a sizable herd. By then, the war was over. Mother called it a 300-mile mistake. They laughed about it later, but at the time, he thought he had dug a hole he couldn't get out of."

I stopped digging to catch my breath and looked up at Rue. She was sitting on Calvin's headstone, smoking a cigarette.

"When did your Dad die?"

"1927. He caught a cold and never got better. I don't think he wanted to live anymore. He was tired, alone, and couldn't work. I was sending him a little money every month, and he hated that. I got a call late one night and left for home immediately. The journey to Utopia over rough, dirt roads took well over eight hours. When I got home, there were several cars and horses in the yard. I was exhausted from the drive, but my emotions would not allow me to rest."

"The house was quiet. The front room had been cleared of all the furniture. My father's coffin rested on two sawhorses near the front window. I sat in a chair next to him. Through the glass, I could see a thin moon and a wide sweep of stars hanging over the ground. My father would often stand in that same spot and look at the sky and the clouds, and like perhaps every farmer and rancher in Texas, wonder why God wasn't more charitable with his rain."

"The Adventists believe that when a person dies, their spirit goes into a holy state called soul sleep. The soul leaves the body and is suspended, somewhere between heaven and earth, until the day the Redeemer returns and reunites their body with their spirit. My father rarely spoke of his spiritual beliefs, but I don't believe he was a true Adventist. He attended church with my Mother to keep peace in the family. The world is what it is, he would say, no more, no less."

I jabbed the shovel into the ground and heard the metal blade hitting something solid.

"Careful now," Rue said. "Don't use the shovel, you'll break it."

I got down on my knees and pulled loose dirt out of the hole with both hands. Then my fingers felt something smooth. A glass jar. I dug around the jar, lifted it out of the ground, and held it up in the moonlight. It was a Mason jar smeared with dirt. I tried to open it, but the lid was rusted shut.

"Just crack it open," Rue said.

I set the jar down, picked up the shovel, and came down hard on the glass. Gold and silver coins and pieces of shattered glass glowed in the moonlight. I stood there, not believing what I was seeing.

Rue stepped close and put her arm around me. "It's all yours, boy. I couldn't bring myself to give it all to Calvin."

27

I read a lot. Helps me escape the hassles and stress of new schools, new towns, and the pain of meeting new people. I love newspapers. I like the way stories are condensed down to the basics. Who, what, when, where, why. Every morning, a fresh disaster, the latest emergency, or nasty scandal, delivered right to your front door. And the next day everything starts over again. A never-ending cycle of misfortune and tragedy. The world's grief and pain conveniently transformed into my entertainment.

When Rue and I got back to the boardinghouse, the sun was just above the tree line. A newspaper was on the front porch. I opened it and scanned the front page. The astronauts were on their way back from the moon. But they were still in considerable trouble. Hundreds of thousands of miles from Earth and short on oxygen. Would they make it back? Or would they run out of air and suffocate, their capsule floating off into empty space?

We went inside and sat at the table. The woman who ran the boarding house poured coffee and set a plate of biscuits in front of us. When she stepped back into the kitchen, Rue handed me a small cloth bag holding all the coins. "Take these to our room and hide them."

When I came back downstairs, Milly and Cora were sitting across from Rue. They were all laughing.

"Rue was telling us about her boyfriend," Cora said.

Rue shook her head. "When a woman is older than sixteen, she doesn't have boyfriends, she has gentleman companions."

"Ok," Cora said, "have it your way. Gentleman companion."

Rue was smiling, in a good mood. "After Calvin was gone, I sold the big house and moved out into the country, a few miles from town. Had a big garden, a few chickens, and goats. There was a small barn on the property. I had a horse I'd ride into town occasionally. And because Calvin took his own life, there was no insurance payout, so I got a job at the library in town."

"How old were you?" I said.

"Stop interrupting me. I don't remember how old I was. Does it matter? I guess I was close to fifty. Now keep your mouth shut and listen." She paused. "You made me lose my story..."

"You were living a few miles from town..." Cora said.

"Right. One day, I look out the window and see this old Ford sedan driving up my road, and there's a horse on a lead tied to the bumper. The Ford stops in front of my place, and an older gentleman climbs out. Living by yourself, you become a little uneasy when a stranger rolls up to your front door. I wasn't frightened, but I prefer caution. I picked up my shotgun by the door and stepped out onto the porch.

"A thin, dark-skinned man with gray hair was standing in my yard, hat in hand, a big smile on his face. He introduced himself as Tio Honeycutt, then he turned and introduced his horse, Miss Libby. He asked if I knew about the races in town in the next few days. It was Texas Independence Day, and there was always a picnic in the park, music, speeches… and horse races. I told him I knew about the celebration. He asked if I would rent him a stall in my barn for a few days, just until after the races.

"Miss Libby won't be any trouble," he said, "I'll feed and water her and muck out the barn for you." "Is she fast?" I said.

"Yes, ma'am," he said, "undefeated."

"Sometimes you just get a feeling about someone. There's no making sense of it. I suppose, looking back on my history with men, I should have been more wary. But I'm glad I wasn't. He asked how much I charge for boarding his horse.

"A dollar a day," I said.

"He got the horse settled in the barn and drove off. The next morning, he was at my place early. He brushed and saddled the horse, then rode her up and down my road for over an hour. After a while, my curiosity took over. I walked out to the road and asked him why he was riding the horse if the race was in a few hours?

"Miss Libby has too much spirit, too much heart," he said. "She does her best racing only after she's run about ten miles."

"I asked if he would like to come into the house for breakfast. He took off his hat and looked at me. I guess he was trying to see what kind of feeling he got from me.

"I won't come inside, ma'am," he said, "but I would take a meal on your porch."

"Tio was a horse trader and a gambler. He'd been everywhere, done all kinds of racing, won a lot of money, lost most of it, and was on his way to being flush again. Miss Libby was his winning ticket.

"Every cowboy in Texas thinks he has a fast horse," Tio said, "and he's willing to risk his wages to prove it. And if money is short, he'll bet a pair of boots, or a truck, or the deed to his land. Quick as a boy climbs on a horse, he's thinking about racing."

"Miss Libby wasn't much to look at, a short, dark sorrel with a wide back. I asked Tio how he knew when she was ready to race.

"If her ears are going every which way," he said, "she's getting ready to buck. If her ears are standing straight up, she's listening. And if those ears are laid back, she's ready to bust loose."

"Tio had found Miss Libby pulling a junkman's cart over in East Texas. The man who owned her was glad to be rid of her, as she'd already destroyed most of his barn. When Tio first saw her, she was tied up in a pasture, far away from any wooden fence or stall she might kick into splinters. But there was something about the horse he liked.

"Miss Libby is a horse from a hundred years ago," Tio said, "she needs to be ridden all day, every day. And when she isn't, she takes it out on whatever is within reach."

"When he finished eating, he stood up and thanked me for the meal and asked if I would be attending the races." "I can't wait to see her run," I said.

"I decided to walk into town. It was a beautiful day, and the wildflowers were just beginning to bloom. When I got to town, a crowd was already gathering around the horses. It was a five-horse race down the length of Main Street, threequarters of a mile from the feed co-op to the courthouse. I saw Tio holding Miss Libby and walked over. He removed his hat, nodded, and asked if I might hold his hat and wallet during the race.

"Do you trust me?" I said.

He smiled, "I guess I'll have to."

"The local champion was a horse named Honcho, owned by a prominent rancher and ridden by his son. Honcho was a long-legged, black thoroughbred, at least a foot taller in the withers than Miss Libby. When I saw the black horse standing quietly in the street, held by the young man, I began to wonder about Tio's confidence. The riders mounted their horses and trotted to the end of the street. The sheriff walked to the middle of the road and put a hand to his eyes. At the far end of the road, a man raised a bandana, signaling that the horses and riders were ready. The sheriff raised his pistol and shot into the air. A cheer exploded from the crowd.

"Folks were already five deep at the finish line, so I walked down the sidewalk away from the mob to get a better look. The black horse was already out front, the others trailing close behind. I couldn't see Miss Libby. The cheering grew louder as the horses approached the courthouse. Then I saw Tio's head. Miss Libby was running just off the big horse's haunches. In the last stretch before the courthouse, she shot forward, and Tio bent low over her neck. They crossed the finish line a few feet ahead of the thoroughbred. The noisy crowd suddenly went quiet.

"I waited until Tio collected his winnings, then walked over and handed him his hat and wallet. "She doesn't like to lose," he said. We walked back to my house, Tio leading Miss Libby, letting her cool down slowly. I asked if he would be staying for a few days. He shook his head.

"Once you've separated folks from their money," Tio said, "it's best to leave town for a while."

"He had business in San Antonio for a few days, and I convinced him to leave Miss Libby in my barn until he returned. That spring and summer, if there was a race within a hundred miles of Utopia, I was there watching Miss Libby run. She won enough races so Tio could trade his old Ford for a new truck and a horse trailer. We traveled as far as Oklahoma City and Santa Fe to race her. She rarely disappointed.

"What about Tio?" Milly said. "Did he disappoint?"

Rue smiled. "Tio and I… became close. That's all I'll say about that."

"What happened to him?" I said.

"He wanted to see California, and I wanted to visit Percy, so we took a road trip out West. We were passing through Nevada, and he read in the paper that the government was testing an atomic bomb in a few days. Turned out we were only a hundred miles from the test site. The paper said it was perfectly safe if you wore sunglasses and stayed back several miles. So, we drove up to Yucca Flat and found a motel room in this little town nearby. The bomb was scheduled for six-thirty the next morning. I called the front desk and asked them to wake us before the bomb. The phone rang early the next morning. We stepped outside in our pajamas, put on our sunglasses, and waited. It was early dawn, the air was cool, and the desert was quiet. And then there was a bright flash like the sun had fallen out of the sky and a rumble under our feet like the earth was breaking open. Seconds later, the air began to vibrate. I was scared and grabbed Tio's hand. Then it was quiet and still again. We went back inside, dressed, and when we came out, there was a fine layer of dust on everything. But it wasn't dust, it was a gray metallic ash. We had to use the wipers to clear the windshield.

"When we got back to Texas, Tio moved in with me. I didn't care what everyone in town was saying. Miss Libby was retired by this time, free to run around all day in my pasture. Tio was on the lookout for his next horse, driving all over the state, talking to traders. When he came home from one of his trips, he had a cough.

Rue paused and took a deep breath. "He was gone by the end of the year."

28

I was standing on Mateo's porch looking east. The sun was down, the stars were beginning to blink on. Everyone else was inside eating and drinking. The old guy was a little drunk, slouched in a chair, a bottle of beer in his hand. Telling me about the old days.

"The last drives were in the late forties," he said. "I was a cowboy back then until the drought drove me into town. Now I work for the city. Oh well…what you gonna do?"

He struggled to rise from the chair. "I wanna show you something." He stumbled inside and came out holding a dark rock the size of a baseball. He handed it to me.

"I was on the midnight to dawn watch," he said, "just me and about five hundred restless cows. The night was like this, clear, lots of stars. I was looking at a particularly bright one a few degrees above the western horizon. Kept getting bigger and brighter, then this blast of light flashed across the sky, and I heard a loud boom. I thought the world might be ending, so I said a prayer. Said a lot of prayers. The thing had a long tail of fire, streaked right over my head, and plowed into the trees. My horse started spinning in circles, making all kinds of noise. Took me a while to settle her down. When she was calm, I rode over to where the thing had started a small grass fire. I realized the world wasn't ending, and I thought perhaps God was trying to tell me something. But I didn't hear any voices or anything, no angels appeared. Just this rock jammed into the ground. I stomped out the fire and bent down to look at it. Pretty ordinary, just a rock. Tried to pick it up, but it was too hot to touch. When it cooled, I put it in my bag and carried it home. I look at it every day, waiting for a sign. A burning rock falls out of the sky after traveling a million miles and lands at your feet…gotta be a message in that."

Gabby and Cora walked onto the porch with their arms around each other.

"He says you see ghosts, Matty," Cora said.

Gabby shook his head, "That's not what I said." He pulled her close, kissing her on the cheek. "Tati, tell her about your uncle."

Mateo took a long drink from the bottle. "For many years, my uncle repaired shoes at the back of a laundry in San Antonio. A few days after he passed, I found my boots by the front door. Which was odd, cause I always kept 'em at the back of my closet. One of the soles had a hole in it. It was my uncle telling me to get the boots fixed."

"Your uncle's ghost moved the boots," Cora said.

"No ghost," Matty said. "My uncle looked after me when he was alive. Why wouldn't he do the same after he was gone?"

Rue and Frederic came out on the porch to say goodbye. Rue put her arms around me. I shook hands with Frederic.

"First, his daughter runs away," Rue said, "then his Mother abandons him, and now his son cuts out for the Wild West. Your old man is gonna pitch a fit." She put her hands on my face and pulled me close. "Remember, boy. You're skating on thin ice, so keep moving as fast as you can."

Milly came outside with her camera and lined us up on the porch. Matty, Rue, Frederic, Cora, Gabby, and me. She pushed the red button, and a blank picture emerged. Matty took it from Milly and looked at the blank space, waiting for the image to be revealed.

"Memories…ghosts," Matty said, "same thing."

29

My emotions seemed to be sabotaging my thinking. I tried to consider the situation with Milly, but couldn't manage it. I kept seeing images of her and Shade, or Cora kissing her, the night of the dog fight. I knew I wanted to be with her, but I had no clue how she felt about me. I decided not to tell Milly about the bag of coins. If I were going on the run, I'd need money, and I wasn't sure how long she would stick around. I had to start thinking about what to do next, where to go.

It was late morning when I came downstairs for breakfast. Frederic and Rue had left early for the airport. Cora had decided to delay her return to Louisiana for a while. Gabby and Matty had invited her to stay as long as she wanted. Milly was sitting on the porch looking at a roadmap. I stepped outside and sat down.

"It's a big country," Milly said, looking up. "Lots of places to hide."

"You got any ideas…I mean, where should we go?"

"We're here." She put a finger on the map and traced a route out of Texas, through New Mexico, Arizona, Colorado, up into Utah, and then into Wyoming. "And in a few days we could be here."

"What's that?"

"Yellowstone."

We put our bags in the Caddy and drove away from Utopia, Milly behind the wheel. It was a warm day, a clear blue sky. Gradually, we left the rolling green hills and cedar trees around Utopia and entered a dry flatland of mesquite trees, sage, and sand. Texas is a big state with so many different kinds of terrain. We passed through Junction, Sonora, Ozona, Fort Stockton, Van Horn, and late in the afternoon entered the outskirts of El Paso, the far western edge of the state. We were both tired and hungry, but neither of us wanted to stop. We hit a drive-thru Mexican restaurant and kept going north. It was almost midnight when we rolled into Albuquerque.

Milly found a cheap motel west of the city, and we dragged ourselves into the room and fell on the bed. We'd barely spoken to each other all day. The uncertainty of my situation was beginning to sink in. Life on the run, no stable home, no family. Lying on the bed in the dark, staring at the ceiling, I wasn't sure I could do it. How long would I have to run? Forever? Or just until the war was over? I reached out and took Milly's hand. I was scared and just wanted to touch someone. She pulled her hand away and sat up.

"Listen to me, Jim. I don't want to be alone right now, and you're the only person I can stand to be around. But that's as far as it goes. Understand?"

I nodded.

She went into the bathroom, and the shower came on. I closed my eyes, and when I opened them again, it was morning, and Milly was gone. I panicked, dressed quickly, and stepped outside. The Caddy was still there, covered in dust, the windshield smeared with flattened bugs.

I looked up to see her crossing the gravel parking lot holding a paper bag and two coffees. "You thought I'd left you, didn't you?"

"Just for a second."

She handed the bag and a coffee.

"If I'm going to leave you, I'll let you know."

"I guess that's comforting…sort of."

She lit a cigarette and reached into the bag for a donut.

"Breakfast of champions," she said.

We drove west toward Arizona. The land was flat, empty, covered in green sage and dry grass. The low gray clouds, in the distance, looked like mountain ranges. Later in the day, as the sun moved higher in the sky, the clouds burned off, and real mountains rose abruptly from the level plain. We stopped in Flagstaff for lunch and wandered into a sporting goods store.

"We need to save our money," Milly said. "Quit staying at motels. We can sleep outside at state parks, campgrounds."

"I've never slept outside before.

"Jesus." She shook her head. "I worry about you, Jim. You are on the run from the law. You need to get real. If they catch you, you're going to jail."

We bought two sleeping bags, a small tent, a Coleman stove, a cooking pot, two spoons, two plastic lawn chairs, and a hatchet.

Milly wanted to sleep, so I got behind the wheel. We climbed up through the red hills outside Flagstaff, heading west, then north towards Page, Arizona. The landscape was unbelievable, like nothing I had ever seen. Massive red cliffs looming over the road and beyond the cliffs, dry treeless plateaus extending for miles. At the extreme edge of the horizon was a range of blue mountains, the peaks covered in snow. Milly slept most of the day, and late in the afternoon, I drove into Zion National Park. We set up our tent under the trees in an empty campground and walked to a nearby store for supplies.

The next morning, we climbed to the top of one of the massive walls of red rock. Steps had been carved into the face of the cliff. At the top of the cliff, a small clearing overlooked vast canyons of stone. Strong currents of cool air rushed skyward over the face of the red rock. At the bottom of the canyon, a thin road ran beside a silver river. It felt like the clouds were just above our heads. We sat on a rocky perch for hours, neither of us saying a word, watching the clouds change shapes. Dark shadows moved across the faces of the rock as the sun rolled across the sky. Birds hung motionless in the currents.

Later that afternoon, we packed up our gear, and I drove north. The entire state appeared to be nothing but a large pile of red rocks with a few farming towns set back against dry cliffs. Since leaving Utopia, the sky seemed to have expanded, grown into this vast blue space, an overpowering presence, a constantly changing spectacle of clouds and wind and light. We stopped in Filmore for lunch and kept moving. Milly was driving now, and I was searching the roadmap for campgrounds.

"What's that?" Milly said, pointing to a line of low red clouds off to the west

"Could be mountains."

"I don't think so. It wasn't there ten minutes ago."

She turned on the radio, trying to get a weather report. Nothing but static. She turned it off.

"That's a storm," she said, "but why is it red?"

The red clouds, lying flat across the terrain, were growing rapidly in size. We watched the dark wall move closer, across the empty terrain, toward the highway. Gusts of wind began to shake the car. Lightning lit up the red clouds. Then the force of the storm hit the Cadillac, pushing it onto the shoulder of the road. Milly struggled to keep the car on the highway. Clouds of red dust engulfed the vehicle. Only a few feet of road were visible through the swirling dirt. Powder-fine dust streamed in through the vents.

"I gotta get off the road," Milly said. "I can't see shit."

She guided the Caddy to the shoulder of the highway and stopped.

Wind blasted hard against the windows. The red dust was so thick it felt like we were inside a blender. A car rolled slowly by, then another, and then a large truck zoomed past, and seconds later, we heard the sound of metal colliding with metal.

"Slow down, people," Milly yelled.

Cars kept coming up behind us, disappearing in the red dust and then slamming into the cars up ahead. The inside of the Caddy was covered in a fine red powder. I could taste the dirt with each breath. Thick red clouds blocked out the sun. The light dimmed.

After a few hours, the storm began to weaken, and we could see the sky again. A flashing red light appeared behind us. A sheriff's car rolled slowly down the highway. We could see the dim outline of the accident in the distance. A truck had jack-knifed across the road, and dozens of cars had plowed into the truck. The wreckage spread across both lanes of the highway. A few people were out of their cars, looking at the damage.

"Should we see if we can help?" I said.

Milly shook her head. "We're gonna help ourselves."

She turned the Caddy around and headed back to Filmore on the shoulder of the highway. We passed tow trucks and then an ambulance with the siren wailing. We found a cheap motel by the highway, had a pizza delivered to the room, and sat on the bed watching Godzilla with the sound off. A giant radioactive lizard destroys a city.

Milly fell asleep, and I went out for a newspaper. The storm had passed, leaving a thick haze of red dust hanging in the air. A fat, red moon hung over the dark mountains. On the front page of the paper was a picture of the three astronauts waving to a crowd. They'd made it home safely.

Well, at least someone is safe, I thought.

30

We headed north on the interstate toward Scipio, then took the state road to Salina. Milly was driving. She wanted to get off the interstate highways. Too much traffic, too many cops, she said.

The empty state road ran down the center of a small valley bordered on both sides by steep green hills. There were no houses, fences, or barns. A few cows grazed among the sage. Red dust still hung in the air from the storm, turning the sun into a glowing pink ball. In more than an hour, we never saw another car. The only sign of civilization was an actual sign: Open Range.

"What does that mean?" I asked.

"It means watch out for cows on the highway."

We both saw it at the same time, a dark shape in the road. As we got closer, we saw a man pushing a shopping cart down the middle of the highway. Milly slowed down and pulled up alongside him. The man was badly sunburned on his face and arms; his long, dirty hair was tied back with a bandana. There was an old guitar and a few books in the cart.
He stopped and looked at us.

"Are you ok, mister?" I said.

"What day is this?" He asked.

"Tuesday."

"What month?"

"April."

"I assume we are still struggling through the year 1970."

"When was the last time you had something to eat?" Milly said.

He considered the question, then said, "I had a candy bar a few days ago. Ran out of water this morning." He held up an empty plastic bottle.

I helped him load his bulky shopping cart into the Caddy's huge trunk. I had to tie the trunk down with a rope to keep it shut. The man climbed into the back seat with his guitar, leaned against the door, and fell asleep.

When we stopped for gas, the stranger woke up, climbed out of the Caddy, stretched, and looked around. Across the highway from the gas station was a diner, with a few trucks parked out front. Milly asked the man if he was hungry. He nodded.

We walked across the highway, went inside, and slid into a booth next to a window. A waitress came to the table to take our order.

"Get whatever you want, it's on us," Milly said.

He ordered two breakfasts and coffee. Milly and I ordered pancakes. When the food arrived, the man held out his hands and asked if we would join him in saying grace. I thought he might be some kind of religious nut, wandering the roads of Utah. I was ready for a long prayer. Instead, we joined hands, and he said, "Rub a dub dub, thanks for the grub. Go God go, amen.

Cutting the eggs and bacon into small bite-sized portions, he ate slowly and methodically, chewing his food thoroughly. The man was in no hurry. He smiled the whole time. I had questions, but decided to wait until he finished. When the plates were empty, he pushed them to the center of the table and sat back.

"Could I bum a cigarette?"

Milly lit one and handed it to him. He took a deep drag and blew the smoke over our heads.

"What are you doing way out here?" I said. "Pushing a shopping cart?"

He extended a hand across the table. "Francis Tate. Pleased to meet you."

I shook his hand and told him my name.

"And who is your lovely companion, Mr. Birdwell?"

"Milly. No need for last names." She leaned forward. "I know you've got a story. Let's hear it.

Francis took a drag on the cigarette and looked out the window. "The army released me back into society after fifteen months at war. I was like a wild animal. The only skill I possessed was killing people. I was very good at my job, but it was of limited use back in the world. So I picked up the guitar. Thought it might be good for my head, my soul. Got an apartment in Los Angeles, a job as a delivery driver, and lived a quiet life. Then I met this black dude who was also making music, with a great voice. Charles cracked me up. His motto was: Make haste, but slowly."

He took another hit on the cigarette. "LA being LA, my man Charles knew a guy who knew a guy who hooked us up with an agent. Next thing we know, we're in the studio making music. A few months later, the album is released, gets some solid airplay, and our agent tells us it's time to go on the road. Charles and I pull together a small band and start doing gigs up and down the West Coast. Traveling minstrels we were, the last of the hardcore troubadours. Sleeping with strangers, making money, eating drugs."

The waitress came to the table and cleared the plates.

Francis waved the cigarette while he talked. "The music business attracts a certain type of individual. Men and women who have the personality, the talent, and the flexible morals suited to the industry's special requirements. But a man can only do so much before he puts his soul in peril. I felt my spirit spiraling down to nothing. There were sharks everywhere, and at night, the zombies came out. We were making lots of money, but for who? After a year on the road, we decided to take a break, decompress, and get back to normal. Whatever that is. Then they killed Dr. King and Bobby, and it felt like evil was winning. I had what you might call an epiphany, a spiritual vision. I was tripping my brains out sitting on my balcony, watching the setting sun go through numerous color changes, and I realized that God had made the world both light and dark, but that somehow the balance had shifted toward dark. The Lord was faced with a dilemma. He could either let His creation descend into wickedness, or He could destroy this beautiful world He had so wondrously made."

"Are you some kind of preacher?" I said.

"I'm not a preacher, but anyone who understands animals knows that when a creature is suffering, you must end its pain. And this world is suffering. Look around you, son. God is putting this shameful world out of its misery."

We were quiet. Francis finished his cigarette and stubbed it out.

"Where's your home?" I said.

"Right now, my home is the scriptures. Do you read the
Bible, son?"

"Once in a while."

"Read it. The good book is an owner's manual for a righteous life."

"Don't you miss your old life?" Milly said.

"I have my music. And God provides everything else.

"We paid for this meal," Milly said.

Francis smiled. "But the Lord moved your spirit to do so."

We drove north on Highway 89. Francis leaned against the door with the guitar in his lap. Whatever song we called out, he played it. It was like having a jukebox in the back seat.

He had a nice, calming voice, like an urgent whisper. Francis was working on a song about his life. From soldier to musician to wandering pilgrim. The only line I remember was:

I went from rags to riches to sleeping in ditches.

In the little town of Axtell, he put down the guitar, looked around, and asked Milly to stop the car. "This is as good a place as any," he said.

Francis and I pulled the shopping cart out of the trunk while Milly went inside a small grocery store. She came back with a wide-brim straw hat, three Snickers bars, and a canteen.

"Try to stay out of the sun," she

said "I will. And thank you for the

meal."

"How long are you going to keep doing this?" I said.

Francis put the hat on and looked up at the blue sky, the fat white clouds.

"The Jews wandered in the desert for forty years before they understood God."

31

We stayed on Highway 89, going north, up through Salt Lake City and finally into Idaho. The mountains faded to the horizon, and all around us were rolling grassy plains and the metal booms of giant irrigation machines crawling across the vast, dry landscape. We passed through small farming towns separated by miles of open, empty prairie. It was getting dark; the clouds were turning red in the west. Milly was driving. She looked tired

"Where are we going?" I said.

"Yellowstone…remember?"

"No, I mean…where are we going, our destination?"

"Well, Montana seems like a good idea. Lots of space up there. We'll find a nice little cowboy town, change our names, and get a driver's license. We need to lay low until this country comes to its senses." She smiled at me. "You can learn to be a cowboy. Take up hunting and fishing. Maybe have the childhood you didn't get."

We were quiet for some time, then Milly said, "You worried about how all this is gonna play out?

I almost told her about the gold coins, but I hesitated.

"This is new to me," I said. "Running from the law, living on my own.

"What scares you the most?"

"I'm not afraid. To be afraid, I'd need something in my life I was scared of losing."

"What about your family?"

"After Nancy left, my family just kind of fell apart. Rue is the only thing holding us together…now she's gone." I looked at her; she seemed sad.

"Are you ok?" I said

Milly rested her chin on the steering wheel. "All I got is nothing, and I'm running out of that."

The rest of the afternoon I lay on the backseat and looked at the sky through the back window. The clouds looked like enormous seashells resting underwater. The rippled textures and uniform patterns were shaped by the wind. Clouds streamed out of my view, and all I could see was the sky, the brilliant light flooding the inside of the car. It felt like we were floating, riding up and down the dry hills, a boat drifting on the waves.

I looked out the window at the passing terrain and tried to imagine this land as a single continuous country. From the East Coast, traveling west across the green fields of the Midwest, through grasslands and forests, over the dry plains and prairies, then up and over the mountains and across the desert to the ocean. How could a nation this vast be one country?

But this country wasn't just a single cohesive entity; it was a chaotic, messy multitude. Maybe the secret to staying out of jail or the army was finding a quiet, uninhabited corner of America with lots of space to spread out and live whatever life was required. The Caddy was gently rocking and swaying. I closed my eyes and fell asleep.

We stopped at a campground near Earthquake Lake in Idaho. The man running the campground took our money and pointed us to a spot at the far end of the lake. He told us the lake had been formed ten years ago when an earthquake caused a landslide, blocking the river and creating a wide body of water. The campground was empty except for a yellow VW van.

Milly parked the Caddy, set up our tent, crawled inside, and fell asleep.

I wasn't sleepy, so I took a hike around the lake. The blue sky was fading into the night; the air was cool. A large flock of starlings flew across the surface of the lake. The swarm rose and twisted, spinning skyward in the thin light above the water. The swooping birds were like a dark floating wave. There were thousands of them, wing-to-wing, chattering. The swarm changed shapes as it rose and fell and rose above the flat water.

I couldn't move; I felt like the world was trying to tell me something. Thousands of birds were performing some kind of spontaneous, instinctive ritual. It had to mean something.

The bird cloud flowed and shifted, rising high above the lake, squawking louder now, a roaring, persistent buzz in the quiet night as the mass of birds flew higher into the sky, then disappeared over the ridge of the mountain.

We woke up in the morning to a few inches of snow. It was cold, and the sun was out. There was a man standing outside the yellow van, drinking coffee. He waved at me. I waved back, and he walked over.

"I have some fresh coffee, if you're interested," he said.

Dale and April were from Southern California and looked to be a few years older than Milly. He poured us coffee while April made a breakfast of pancakes and bacon. The space was tight inside the van, but all four of us fit comfortably. Dale asked where we were heading, and Milly told a nearly truthful story about a funeral in Texas and wanting to see the country.

"This is a great van," I said. "It's got everything."

"Funny story how we got the van," Dale said.

He opened a cabinet at his elbow, pulled out a cigar box, and began rolling a joint.

"I started doing burglaries for this dude Tony when I was still in high school," he said. "Small stuff, mostly residential. Tony used to say stealing is easy, there's no entrance exam, anybody can do it. The hard part was getting rid of the stuff. That's why his cut was sixty to my forty. Then someone shot him, and I had to find a new connection. I was tired of stealing anyway; there was no future in it. I wanted something with a bigger payoff. I thought about banks, but I'd need a partner, someone I could trust. And trust is hard to come by these days.

"Anyway…this guy on my softball team owned an auto repair shop, and he asked me if I could steal a brand new Mercedes 250SL. He wanted to strip it for parts. He was offering five hundred bucks. I'd never jacked a car before, but it didn't look that hard. I knew the perfect spot in Newport. You should have seen the wheels that rolled up to that place. Ferrari, Mercedes, Maserati. The valet would open the door, and some rich bitch would climb out and hand over the keys.

"I waited in the lot until the valet pulled up in the Mercedes I was looking for. Showed him my pistol, not even loaded. Didn't want anyone to get hurt. Hands me the keys, and off I go. I'm cruising up the interstate, it's a beautiful day, sun's out. I decide to hit Oceanside and grab some lunch before I turn over the wheels. I had a few beers and fish tacos and then drove along the beach back toward town. I'm two blocks from the guy's shop, and this cop lights me up. I got two choices: pull over and he takes me to jail, or outrun him. I'm young, my dick is hard, and I'm steel-plated. So I floor it and off we go. It wasn't much of a chase. Ran out of gas before I got to Anaheim. I lucked out at my trial. The judge gave me twenty-four months. I did eighteen up at Mule Creek. I'd never been up north, it's beautiful. Mountains, clean air.

"So I'm on parole, and I joined this religious cult in San Diego. The Sunshine Family. Figured being around godly people would keep me out of trouble. It sorta worked. Their thing was to sell flowers at the airport. Buy the flowers for a dollar, sell 'em for two bucks. I was stoned most of the time. Had to be stoned, waving flowers around all day. Those people scared me, always talking about the end of time, preparing your soul for heaven by eliminating all sin. I didn't know if I wanted to eliminate all my sins. I enjoyed some of them. If drinking and fucking are sins, then count me out, brother.

"I prayed for God to change my life. And one day, he did. The Sunshine Family had this tiny office behind a laundromat where they did all their business. I walked in after my shift at the airport, and the place was empty. Sitting on the desk was the family's cash box. Didn't even think about it. Put it under my arm and drove straight to Mexico. There was over ten thousand bucks in that box. Praise
Jesus."

April took the joint from Milly.

"That's where I met him," April said. "I was hanging out in Ensenada with some friends, and he was skateboarding. He looked good. I got an immediate vibe from him. I had these little cards shaped like a heart. On one side, I wrote: You are a beautiful person. On the other side, I wrote: And so am I. I gave him one of my cards.

"We went to the park and got stoned, and he said he wanted to get his car cleaned, so we went to the car wash. The soap splashing on the windows, those big brushes whipping around. We couldn't help ourselves, we jumped in the backseat and got it on while rolling through the car wash.

It was trippy. I thought, this guy is fun, and I need some fun right now."

I took the joint from Milly.

"I had a little money left," Dale said, "so I bought this van and me, and April decided to see the country. The good parts. You know, look around, find us a place where we can settle down, maybe have a kid. Become real citizens, you know."

We sat in the van talking, and eventually the sun came out and melted the snow. April asked Milly where we were headed next.

"Yellowstone," she said.

April smiled. "That's where we're going."

32

Yellowstone had been open only a week. The roads, the parking lots, the trails, all empty. Except for a few maintenance workers. Seemed like we had the whole place to ourselves. Milly was driving. We followed the yellow van through the northern section of the park, the road running along the edge of Yellowstone Lake. It was a beautiful day; the sun was out, and a few thin clouds were gliding across the sky. The hills, mountains, and meadows were a bright, vibrant green. Blue, churning creeks ran beside the road. Thick pine forests as far as you could see.

Dale turned off the highway, down a dirt road that wound up through a grassy meadow and into the trees. We passed a few signs warning us to turn back: Park Personnel Only.

I looked at Milly. She shrugged. "He seems to know what he's doing."

The yellow van rolled to a stop. Dale got out and walked over.

"Would you like to go for a hike?"

We nodded

"Great. But first, let's get our heads in a good place.

We were all sitting in the van watching a pan of water come to a boil. When it bubbled, April lifted the pan off the stove and poured the water into a small clay teapot. She added a handful of mushrooms to the pot, closed the lid, and said, "It has to steep."

After several minutes, she poured the muddy brown liquid into a large coffee mug and set it on the table. "Now, we let it cool."

April put her hand on Dale's leg. "Let's only put positive thoughts out in the world today," she said.

Dale nodded and picked up the mug. "Think of the most beautiful day you've ever had," he said, and took a big drink.

I tried to think of a happy memory, but nothing immediately came to mind. Then I remembered the trip our family took to San Diego. We stayed at a hotel on the beach. Nancy and I played in the water all day, building sandcastles, collecting shells. When we got hungry, my Dad and I walked to a food shack on the beach and ordered burgers and fries. He stood quietly, smiling, looking out at the blue ocean. Then he put his arm around me and pulled me close. "This isn't too bad," he said.

Dale handed me the mug. I took a drink and handed it to Milly. We passed the mug around until it was empty. April dumped the soggy mushrooms into the pan, and we all ate one.

I filled two canteens while Dale loaded a small bag with apples and oranges.

What I remember of that day is the intensity of the sky and clouds. The vivid green trees and fields. We started up a wide trail that snaked up through thick pine trees. The walking was easy, with the sharp smell of pine and cool air. Milly and April are ahead of us, talking. The sun warmed my face.

The trail moved up through a forest and out into wide grassland with a clear creek flowing down into a small lake. April stopped and looked back. "Milly and I are staying here."

"Fine," Dale said. "Come on, kid."

Dale started up through a stand of trees on the far side of the lake, and that's when things shifted in my head. My brain suddenly seemed unable to assimilate the immense world in front of my eyes. My senses were overloaded; everything seemed magnified. I felt no anxiety about anything, no worry, just an overwhelming feeling of ease and contentment. I couldn't stop smiling.

The dark tree branches crossing overhead looked like open arms, welcoming us. Wind in the leaves sounded like the land was breathing. Birds were singing to each other. I thought if I listened closely enough, I might understand what they were saying.

We stopped at the top of a hill and looked back at the small lake. April and Milly were standing in the water, naked, holding hands.

Dale turned to look at me. "The trees are our friends," he said. He was thinking the same thing I was thinking. How was that possible? I opened my mouth to say something, but the sounds didn't seem to mean anything.

We walked out of the trees and began a slow climb up the ridge of a steep, rocky hill. The top of the ridge was hidden in the clouds. Dale stopped, pulled the canteen out of his pack, and handed it to me. I unscrewed the cap and drank. Water had never tasted so sweet.

The hill was a sharp pyramid of exposed rock rising from the grassy terrain. Soon we were scrambling over boulders, climbing up steep ledges. The peak of the ridge seemed impossibly far away. We were tiny ants moving slowly over the rocky ground. This hill of stone was our home.

The wind picked up, and thick clouds engulfed us, blocking our view of the land. The wet mist made the rocks slippery, and climbing became more difficult. Dale slowed his pace, moving cautiously over the wet slabs of stone. The clouds were so thick I could only see a few feet in front of my sneakers. Dale reached out his hand, guiding me up the steep trail. I felt like we were leaving the solid earth and climbing up into the clouds.

Then, like a curtain opening, the clouds streamed past, and the vast landscape below became visible. Wide expanses of green forest, broad patches of grassy meadows, and wide silver rivers. Creeks cutting through the hills, rocky peaks jutting up from the landscape. The endless blue sky above our heads.

I wasn't an ant any longer. I was a single-cell creature swimming in an immense space, connected to every living thing. We had reached the top of the ridge. I sat down, trying to take it all in. Dale stood on the rocky peak, his hair swirling in the wind, arms above his head like some kind of crazy human antenna.

"Ladies and gentlemen," he screamed, "please fasten your seat belts. We are approaching maximum bliss."

We sat on the ridge for hours, the view under our feet constantly changing. Clouds floated in front of the sun, putting the colors of the landscape below into motion. Flowing from light to shadow. Shiny silver rivers became flat gray bands of shadow. Birds soared up from the ground, weightless, on rising currents.

We ate the apples and oranges and drank what was left in the canteen. Neither one of us spoke for most of the afternoon. We watched the earth turn, the clouds and wind moving over the landscape, the sun sliding toward the horizon. After a long while, the light began to soften.

Climbing down was slow going. The rocks were wet and mossy. At times, the trail led us along the edge of a steep drop. Strong currents rushed up from the ground. Dale stopped often to wait for me or to offer his hand.

Hours later, we were back on relatively level ground. We walked back through the forest and down to the small lake. The sun was low over the hills when we spotted the yellow van parked in the shade. A thin line of smoke rose through the trees.

As we approached the campfire, the women looked up at us. They were both still naked, wearing only sneakers. Milly was standing up, holding a wooden walking stick. April was crouched at the fire, roasting a marshmallow on a twig. They looked like wild animals that had wandered into our camp.

I couldn't stop looking at Milly. Her legs and arms were sunburned and scratched, her hair wet, matted with leaves and grass.

"What have you guys been up to?" Dale said.

"We were running through the trees," Milly said.

"Did you catch anything?" I said.

"We weren't trying to catch anything," she said. "We were just running."

April looked up and offered me a marshmallow. I put it in my mouth. It was hot and sweet and sticky and smoky. April stood up, and I noticed a bluebird tattoo on her ankle. I must have still been high because the bird moved up her leg, glided across her belly, and disappeared into the trees. I turned to ask Dale if he had seen the bird. He was staring at
Milly.

I woke up sometime in the night. Milly wasn't in her sleeping bag. I unzipped the tent flap and looked out. The bright yellow moon reflected on the calm lake. There was a faint glow coming from the van. I crawled out of the tent and walked over quietly. The curtains were pulled tight over the windows, but through a small gap I saw Dale's naked back, his shoulder muscles flexing slowly. It was quiet except for a low, excited moan.

The next morning, I crawled out of the tent and stretched. Dale was standing by a fire, holding a coffee mug.

"There he is," he said, "back from the dead."

I walked over. He poured coffee into a mug and handed it to me.

"How'd you sleep, kid?

"Fine. I guess. My brain feels a little fuzzy."

I looked at him. Light brown hair down to his shoulders, bright, clear eyes. He was smiling.

Of course, he's in a good mood, I thought, he's been fucking two women all night.

I couldn't name what I was feeling at that moment, but I didn't like it. Jealousy? Envy? Was there a difference?

"Where's Milly and April?" I said.

"They took a walk."

It was quiet by the lake, the water flat and still. The cold morning air. A wall of thick evergreens surrounded the water.

"Milly tells me you just got your draft notice."

I nodded.

"So what's your plan? Mexico or Canada?"

"Not sure. Still doesn't seem real."

Dale took a sip of coffee. "Just imagine what would happen if the government decided to draft all the pet dogs in America and send 'em to war. Folks would riot in the streets. But tell people their sons need to go ten thousand miles to the other side of the world to kill commies cause it's their patriotic duty…well, that's fine."

I looked at him. "How do you make love to two women at the same time?"

He looked at me to see if I was serious. "You take it slow…and don't rush things."

"Wasn't April jealous?"

"April doesn't own me, and I don't own her. Milly said you two weren't together so…"

"We're not together. We're just traveling together."

"You dig her, don't you? But she doesn't dig you, right?" I nodded.

"That's a tough one, kid. Don't know what to tell you. Maybe start with someone in your own league and work up to Milly."

Dale opened the back of the van and began to set up a small stove. He quickly scrambled some eggs, laid strips of bacon on a hot skillet, and made more coffee. He was talking the whole time.

"I read a lot while I was inside. I won't say I'm educated or anything, far from it. But I learned a few things about people. Most men get excited through their eyes; they're voyeurs. You know what a voyeur is, right?" I nodded.

"Men get turned on by the look of women. Their face, their skin, their hair. Most women, on the other hand, get off on being observed. They enjoy it when someone
compliments their looks, their style."

He turned to look at me. "I guess that's why men like porn and women prefer makeup."

33

It was late morning when we got all our gear loaded into the Caddy. We made plans to meet Dale and April in a week's time. Noon at the post office in Clearwater, Montana.

April gave Milly a hug. Dale stepped close, put a hand on Milly's back, and kissed her on the cheek. I felt sick.

We drove through the park, out the northern gate, and into Montana. I was quiet most of the day. We stopped for gas in Pray, Montana. Steep mountains on both sides of the highway, a strip of blue sky between the sharp ridges. Milly filled up the tank, climbed in the Caddy, and looked at me.

"You haven't said anything all day. What's the matter?"

"Why did you sleep with Dale and April?"

"Don't get uptight about that."

"I'm not uptight. I just want to know why?"

She smiled at me. "I was feeling good, we'd had a nice day together, and they asked me to join them."

"That's it?"

"That's it. It's not complicated."

"You had sex with someone you just met because you felt like it?"

"That's the only good reason to have sex. If you're not feeling it, don't do it."

"They didn't ask me."

She paused, then said, "No…they sure didn't."

Milly wheeled the Caddy out onto the empty road and accelerated up the highway. We were both quiet for miles.

"Let's get something to eat," she said. "You hungry? I'm starving."

My eyes were burning. I could feel my tears.

Milly reached over and took my hand. "Look, I'm not going to give you any advice about sex. That would imply I know what the fuck I'm doing. Which is certainly not the case."

She took a deep breath and exhaled. "Sometimes sex is like a magic spell, and sometimes it's as ordinary as folding your laundry. Some people are pigs; others are delightful. The trick is finding out which is which before you get in bed with them. Sometimes you're so lonely all you want is a warm body next to you. Sometimes you get this bone-deep, sweaty urge, and you know the next person that walks through the door is in big trouble. Sometimes sex is like a buffet with all your favorite desserts, and you haven't eaten in days. Sometimes sex is another way of saying, Hey, it's really nice to meet you.

Sometimes sex is the answer that makes all those stupid questions disappear."

34

My sister Nancy used to sneak out of the house at night and meet her boyfriend, Gary. Our house had a low roof line and was surrounded by tall oak trees. She would open her window, walk across the roof to the garage, grab a limb, and drop to the ground. My father is a deep sleeper, and my Mother was usually out cold, so they didn't hear anything.

Nancy would tell me later what they'd done for hours in the middle of the night. Driving around smoking cigarettes, listening to the radio, and talking about where they wanted to run away to. Either California or Florida. I never understood why she snuck out of the house to do something so ordinary. I guess it was the thrill of being somewhere she wasn't supposed to be with someone our parents didn't like very much.

Gary was twenty-five, a dropout, and worked at a gas station. Nancy was seventeen, got good grades, and, up until she met Gary, was talking about college. The boyfriend had been to the house a few times for dinner. He'd slouch in his chair, looking bored, and when my old man asked him a question, he'd answer in as few words as possible. And he had long hair. My old man hated long hair. He thought it was some kind of political statement.

Gary was a loser, going nowhere, and my parents never liked him. I guess that was the attraction for Nancy.

The army has some strange policies about dependents. That's what the army calls family members. At times, it felt like our entire family was in the army. For example, when a child of an army officer misbehaved, displaying fairly normal adolescent behavior like being expelled from school or getting busted for shoplifting, the details of their misconduct are called a Delinquent Report. The report was sent to the officer's supervisor. If an officer's kids got more than two DRs, it negatively affected the officer's promotions, their job status, and where they were stationed. The army reasoned that if a man couldn't control his own kids, how could he control soldiers?

Neither one of us had ever had a DR. Not because we hadn't done anything bad, we just hadn't been caught. A few weeks before she left home, Nancy snuck out of the house with Gary, and they were busted for a curfew violation. When the cop looked inside the car, Nancy wasn't wearing any shoes. For some reason, the cop thought this was significant and arrested Gary for attempted statutory rape. Nancy called my dad from the police station. He wasn't happy. The incident would be my old man's first DR.

The next morning, Nancy was sitting at the kitchen table, eating cereal, when I came downstairs. I asked how she was doing, and she shrugged. I think she'd already made up her mind to leave and was just waiting for the right moment. "How's your boyfriend?" I said.

She looked at me and shook her head. "I wouldn't call him my boyfriend. Don't even like him that much…but he has a car."

Milly and I drove north to Livingston, past Bozeman, then took Highway 84 heading west. The road was mostly empty; every once in a while, we passed a pickup pulling a horse trailer. The view was of green, rolling grasslands as far as we could see and, at the edge of the horizon, the pale outline of mountains. Overhead, a vivid blue sky thick with white clouds. The only evidence of civilization was the wire fences running along the edge of the highway and white grain elevators rising up from the flatland, marking a farmhouse or a small town.

We stopped at a burger shack in Norris, Montana, and sat at a picnic table in the shade, eating cheeseburgers and fries. It was late afternoon; a few local ranchers and their families were waiting in line to order food.

"What day is it?" Milly asked.

I had to think. "Tuesday? No wait, Monday."

"Could you see yourself living in a little town like this?"

I looked around. The main street of Norris was two blocks of brick storefronts and a single traffic light. "Maybe something a little bigger. It should have a movie theater at least."

"A movie theater and a library," she said. "The absolute minimum."

"Do you miss your family?" I said.

"All the time."

"Have you ever tried to contact them?"

"Yeah, this one time. I was in New Orleans, and my money was almost gone. Something came over me, a sadness I couldn't shake. Maybe it was the wet, gray weather. Nothing I did could get me up again. I had to see family, my little brother, and my parents. I knew it was dangerous, but I didn't care. Anything was better than this deep loneliness. I felt like I was already in jail, separated from everything and everyone I loved. So I bought a bus ticket to Athens, Ohio.

"I got off the Greyhound and started walking. Everything looked familiar: the streets, the trees, the cars. I felt better almost immediately. I walked to the park across from my house and sat down, trying to get my courage up, trying to imagine what my mom and dad would do when I knocked on their door. My mom would give me a big hug, start crying, and then try to feed me. Dad would welcome me in and then begin one of his lectures. He might even call the cops. I couldn't be sure. My little brother would run to me, probably start crying. He was twelve when I left; he'd be in high school now.

"It was late March and cold, a little snow on the ground. The sun was going down, and the park was empty. The lights went on in my house. I could see my mom in the kitchen fixing dinner. My dad was probably sitting in front of the TV, watching the news. My brother is probably upstairs doing his homework. I got up, walked across the street, and stood on the sidewalk looking at my house.

"Something came over me. I began to see the world the way it was, not the way I wanted it to be. I was suddenly aware of my new reality, and it was horrible. I felt sick, my head was pounding, my stomach churned. I was looking at my old life from a million miles away. I realized I could never go back to it. There wasn't anything to go back to. My family had moved on. I wasn't Milly Fincher anymore, I was a wandering ghost, an uncomfortable memory. I was the shameful family incident no one would ever talk about. I didn't have a home anymore, so I turned and walked away."

Milly pulled over on the side of the highway, reached into her bag, and grabbed her camera. "The light is perfect right now."

She climbed out and pointed the camera at a small white church, set among a wide field of grass. Daylight was fading, putting the wide landscape under a warm glow. I opened the door and stepped out.

Milly lowered the camera. "Am I going crazy, or is that church moving?"

I watched the small white building moving slowly over the grassy field. We climbed in the Caddy and drove down a narrow dirt road and found an old wooden church resting on a long flatbed trailer. A large tractor was pulling the church; several men walked beside the trailer, guiding its slow progress. A group of women dressed in choir robes strolled behind the trailer.

"I need to see this," Milly said.

She parked the Caddy, and we walked over to the floating church. Milly took a few pictures of the small wooden building hovering over the grass, the sun outlining the roof. She asked the men if they'd pose in front of the church, and after some hesitation, they agreed. One of the men waved his hand at the tractor driver, and the church slowed to a stop. The men stood shoulder to shoulder, arms around each other, the setting sun lit up their smiling faces. Milly snapped an image. She thanked the men, then turned to see the group of women watching quietly.

"Why are you moving it?" Milly asked the women.

A tall woman with red hair smiled at her. "We've been raising money for years to build a new chapel," she said. "And we finally reached our goal this Spring. The plan was to tear down the old church and build the new one…but we couldn't bring ourselves to pull it down."

The woman was crying, wiping her eyes on her sleeve. "We love this old place. The Lord has dwelt here for many years; how could we pull down God's house?"

"Would you mind if we walked along with you?" Milly said. "Maybe take a few pictures?"

"Of course, you're more than welcome."

As the church began to roll forward, the red-haired woman turned to the choir. "Number 201," she said. Finding their places next to each other, the women opened their hymnals and began walking. The red-haired woman nodded her head, and the choir began to sing. The procession moved slowly up the dirt road. The church looked like a ship plowing through a sea of grass. I watched as the last of the daylight drained out of the sky, the sun sinking behind the mountains. The choir's hopeful voices sounded lost in the immense landscape.

35

We stopped at a grocery store and bought a cheap cooler, two bottles of wine, and four cans of Chef Boyardee spaghetti.

We camped at a state park on the Madison River. Once again, we had the campground to ourselves. It was too early in the year for camping, I guess. There were low banks of snow under the trees and on the ridges. The sun dropped behind the mountains, and the temperature fell quickly. That night we had spaghetti and drank cheap wine. Sitting around the fire, Milly and I passed a bottle back and forth.

"I wish I'd asked Dale for some weed," she said.

"This wine is doing the trick."

"Are you getting drunk, young man?"

"Let me see your pictures?"

She looked at me. "Why?"

"'Cause I want to see 'em."

"I dunno. You might get all weird. We're having a good time, let's not ruin it."

"I won't get weird...promise."

She dug around in her bag and handed me a thick stack of Polaroids held tight with rubber bands.

The picture on top of the pile was Shade lying in bed smoking a cigarette. Then, an out-of-focus picture of an angry man without a shirt, pointing at the camera. A pair of roller skates on a chair. I held up a picture of a man standing at a railing, smoking, looking out over a flat ocean with sailboats in the distance.

"Who's this?"

"Don't remember. Some guy on a ferry."

Then an image of thick evergreens in the foreground, and in the distance, a mountain glowing pink in the sunset. I held up a picture of a young man sitting on a bed playing a guitar.

"Who's this?"

"That's the kid I told you about in New Orleans."

Then a trolley car in San Francisco. A house on a snowy street at night, the front window glowing with light. A picture of Milly smoking a cigarette, her hand trying to block the camera. Clothes hanging on a line, an arm reaching in from out of the frame. Milly is sitting in a chair, her back to the camera. A picture of me in my sleeping bag. Dale is rubbing Milly's bare feet. The hands of a woman applying polish to her toenails. An open book resting on the hood of a car. An image of Rue in the backseat of the Caddy looking out the window. I held up a picture of Milly's naked back from the waist up, a towel wrapped around her wet hair.

"Who took this one?" I said.

"I don't remember."

"You don't remember?"

"I've been on the run for years, Jim. My memory is a little fuzzy."

Then, a close-up of drops of blood on Cora's white dress. A birthday cake with candles burning. A rainbow over a dark lake. Seashells on wet sand. Troy, Cora, me, and Rue are standing outside the bus station in Houston. Mateo, Rue, Frederic, Cora, Gabby, and I with the sun on our faces. A small white dog on a leash. A close-up of bullet holes in a dryer door.

I put the rubber bands around the stack and handed it back to Milly.

"Where's the rest of them?" I said.

"That's it."

"Those are just the ones you'll show me. I want to see the ones you won't show me."

She shook her head. "I knew you were gonna get weird."

"I want to see all the pictures."

She took a drink from the bottle. "You're too young. You wouldn't understand what you're looking at, and you'd start asking questions, and I don't feel like talking about all that stuff."

"What stuff?"

"Personal stuff, Jim. You don't get to know everything about me."

I grabbed the bottle and took a long drink.

Milly stood up. "I'm going to bed."

I finished the bottle, opened the second bottle, and took a long drink. Then I wandered around the empty campground in the dark. The night sky was huge with millions of stars blazing overhead. The cold air. Silver clouds hang over the outline of the mountains. The overpowering scent of pine trees.

I finished the second bottle, crawled into the tent, and zipped it shut. Milly was asleep. I lay on top of my bag, thinking, struggling to put words to my mental turmoil. My heart was pounding. My brain felt like it was on fire. I reached over and pulled Milly toward me, pushing my face against hers.

She shoved me hard against the tent and shouted, "Stop it or I'll fucking slug you."

"I can do things…the stuff Dale can do."

"You're drunk. Behave yourself…or go sleep outside."

I dragged my sleeping bag out of the tent and crawled into the Caddy. My head churned all night with images of Milly. Things I'd seen or imagined, strange, obsessive dreams.

I watched the sun come up in the back window of the Cadillac, then climbed out and made coffee. I poured a cup and walked over to the tent.

"I have coffee. Would you like some?"

"Sure."

Milly unzipped the tent and stepped out.

"Last night, I was drunk…"

She held up her hand. "Stop. Drunk is an explanation, not an excuse. Let's just forget it."

She sipped the coffee. "I took a philosophy course in my last year at school. All the old Greeks. Socrates, Plato, Democritus. One of them said that the finest love is not for another person but for an idea. I'm in love with the idea of staying out of jail, Jim. My freedom is more precious to me than any person."

36

We stopped for gas and, while Milly filled the tank, I walked over to a phone booth. My hands were shaking when I dropped a quarter into the slot and dialed the number.

After several rings, my Mother's voice said, "Hello."

"It's me…Jim."

"Oh my God…Jim. You're safe. Thank God. Where are you?"

"I just called to tell you I'm fine and that I won't be coming home for a while."

"Some government people came to the house the other day."

"I'm not going to the army, Mom."

"What are you going to do?"

"I don't know…I just know I'm not going to war."

Her voice serious, "I want you to call back in a few hours and talk to your father."

"I don't want to talk to him. I know what he'll say."

"He's worried, son. We both are. You could go to jail." Milly stood by the Caddy, watching me.

"I'll call when I get a chance…" I said.

She had been drinking; her voice drifted slowly out of the phone. "Nancy called. She's living in California now."

"Give me her number."

"I've got it here somewhere…"

I waited while she shuffled papers, then she read the number to me.

"Don't hang up," she pleaded.

"Gotta go…I'll call soon." I hung up.

37

We were driving through the small town in Ennis, Montana, with a few stores, a gas station, and a bar.

"I need to get a few things," Milly said.

She wheeled the Caddy over to the curb, parked in front of a grocery store, and walked inside. When I stepped through the door, Milly was talking to a young guy standing behind the counter. I walked to the back of the store to get a cold drink, and when I turned around, Milly was pointing the pistol at the clerk. My stomach went cold. I ran towards her.

"Milly…no."

The young clerk looked up as the bathroom door opened and a man stepped out. A sheriff's deputy. Everything seemed to slow down. The cop pulled his gun and shouted, "Don't fucking move."

Milly turned, saw the cop, and started to run. The cop yelled again for her to stop. She froze at the door, the gun hanging in her hand.

The young guy behind the counter pointed at me and yelled, "He's with her."

The cop swung his gun toward me, and I raised my hands.

Milly and I stood handcuffed together in the sheriff's office while the deputy phoned his boss. I couldn't look at her.

"Millicent Fincher and James Birdwell," the deputy said. "Both have valid driver's licenses...yeah, I can do that, sheriff...all right...No, I'm on duty all night...I took Carl's shift...I can drive 'em up to Bozeman in the morning, hand 'em over...that's fine." He hung up the phone.

The deputy opened a metal door at the back of the office and led us into a small room with two cells separated by a concrete wall. He put Milly in one cell and me in the other.

No one said a word.

38

Hours later, the door opened, and the deputy walked in holding two trays of food.

"Move to the back of the cell, boy, so I can give you your dinner."

I stepped back, and he slid the tray under the door.

"Step back, hippie," he said to Milly, then pushed the tray under the bars.

"Are you married, Leonard?" Milly said.

"How'd you know my name?"

"Your nametag."

"Oh…right."

"Well…are you married?"

"Shut your fucking mouth, hippie."

"What's your wife's name?"

The deputy stood close to the bars, looking into the cell.

"I'll bet it's DeeAnn or Crystal or…Connie. It's Connie, isn't it?"

The deputy was quiet.

"Once a week, you and Connie get busy, and it's all over in a few minutes."

"Shut up."

"I'll bet she's never even touched it. Bet you've never seen her naked."

"You don't close your mouth, I'll tape it shut."

"Kinky. I like it, Leonard. What else do you have in mind?"

The deputy turned and walked out of the room.

"What are you doing?" I said.

"Trying to get us out of here."

"By pissing him off…you're just making it worse."

I looked down at the tray. Beans, a slice of white bread, and an apple. I slid to the floor. I should have told her about the coins, and none of this would have happened.

"You ok in there?" Milly said.

"What were you doing when you were talking to the deputy?"

"Nothing."

"He was staring at something."

"Was he?"

"Milly…god damn it…what the fuck were you doing?" "Showing him a little tit…get him excited." Her voice was calm. "He's sitting out there at his desk, right now, thinking about me."

I pulled the blanket up and tried to sleep, tried not to think about the next day. This was the end. The deputy would take us to Bozeman, they'd find the warrant on Milly, and she'd go away for a lifetime. If I saw her again, it would be through steel bars or across a table. I'd get several years in a Montana prison if I were lucky. My short life had suddenly boiled down to a single idea. I didn't want to go to prison. I was growing old before I'd had a chance to be young.

I tried talking to Milly, but she wouldn't answer me. I sat in the dark, staring at the concrete wall. I don't remember falling asleep.

Hours later, I opened my eyes when I heard the door open. Light from the outer office spilled across the cement floor. The deputy stood in the doorway. I didn't move, didn't make a sound. He walked to Milly's cell and opened it. From where I was sitting, I could see his figure standing in the open door. The deputy stepped into the cell, disappearing from my view.

"Hey, sweetheart," he whispered.

"I knew you'd come," Milly said quietly.

"This is what you wanted, ain't it?"

It was quiet for several minutes. I could hear his slow breathing, then Milly said, "We'd be more comfortable without this…"

Silence. And then her voice, "That's better, isn't it?"

More deep breathing and then a shout, "No," and a sound like something solid hitting something soft, over and over. The deputy groaned, and it was quiet. Seconds later, Milly was standing at my cell with the key. The door swung open, and I stepped out.

Milly grabbed my hand. "We gotta find the keys to the
Caddy."

"Did you kill him?"

The deputy lay on the floor of the cell, his pants at his knees, blood pooling under his head.

"I can't go to prison, Jim. I'd rather die."

The car keys were in the top drawer of the deputy's desk. The Caddy was parked at the curb outside the sheriff's office.

I drove south on Highway 287, and in a few hours, we were in Idaho Falls. We stopped for coffee and sat in the car watching the sun come up. Neither of us had spoken for hours.

"Do you think he's dead?" I said.

"I don't know. I hit him pretty hard. Let's not talk about
it."

"What do we do now?"

"We gotta get rid of this car. Cops'll be looking for a blue Cadillac."

We found a used car lot off the main highway. Bright plastic flags snapping in the morning breeze. An older man wearing a cowboy hat waved at us as we pulled into the parking lot. He walked over to the Caddy.

"What are you young people looking for?"

"We need a pickup with heavy-duty suspension and four-wheel drive," Milly said.

The old guy had three trucks on his lot fitting that description. An old Dodge flatbed, a rusty blue Chevy, and a bright red, almost new Ford half-ton.

"Which one of these would you drive?" Milly said.

The old guy took off his hat and wiped his forehead. "Not the Dodge, too many miles on it. The Chevy pulls to the right, but you get an alignment, and she'll be good as new."

"What about the Ford?" Milly said.

He shook his head. "A young girl about your age came in here last week, said her husband had passed, didn't need the truck anymore. Took his life in the driver's seat. Tried everything to clean it up. Bleach, Clorox, you name it." "And you think it's haunted or something?" I said.

"Haunted?" he laughed. "Hell no, it ain't haunted. I'm just saying I wouldn't drive it."

I walked over to the Ford and opened the door. There were dark stains across the vinyl dashboard and seats.

"We'll take it," Milly said.

The old man smiled. "Will you folks be paying cash, or do you have something to trade?"

While Milly was inside the sales office doing the paperwork, I reached up under the Caddy's dashboard, grabbed the sack of coins, and stuffed it in my bag.

The old guy gave us a road map of the Western states and an air freshener to hang on the rearview mirror. We threw our gear in the bed of the truck and headed west. I opened the map and looked at the terrain.

"Looks like there are a lot of mountains in Idaho and not a lot of towns. Or we could go north into Canada?"

"I dunno. I need to stop for a few days and get some rest. Think about what to do next."

"I can drive."

She pulled over, and I got behind the wheel. Milly leaned against the window and fell asleep. I kept going west until I hit Highway 93, which ran north through miles and miles of potato fields, straight up into the mountains. In a few hours, we were in Stanley, Idaho.

I was hungry and tired, and I was beginning to see my situation for what it was. I was on the run from the police and wanted by the Draft Board. I pulled into a small diner and went inside. Milly was still asleep in the truck. I didn't wake her. I ordered a cheeseburger and fries and opened the map. Through the diner's window, I could see the jagged peaks of the Sawtooth Range. The name made sense. Steep rocky peaks like the serrated edge of a knife reached into the blue sky. Wide patches of snow still covered the dark faces of the mountains.

I finished my lunch and sat there for a long time studying the map, trying to forget what had happened. My hands felt cold, and my head couldn't make sense of anything. My heart was pounding. I tried to calm my breathing. I stared at the blue sky above the mountains and the thin white clouds and tried to imagine a place where Milly and I were safe.

I ran my finger over the map, drawing a line across the patches of color. This country was an immense place; mountains ran from the southern border, up into Canada, and kept going. We could go to Alaska; there were so many places to get lost up there. The state was mostly unknown, rural, with fewer towns and fewer cops. I traced my finger along a blue highway line that went up the length of Idaho, into British Columbia, and over to Alaska. It would be a long road trip, but we could do it. We had the money.

"What's the plan, Jim?"

I looked up. Milly was standing next to the table.

"Just looking at places, you know, where we could hide."

She sat down, rubbing her eyes. "The first thing we need to decide is whether we should split up or stay together? Cops will be looking for a couple, not two individuals."

I began to panic again. My hands were shaking. "I can't do this alone. Please don't leave me."

She took my hands. "I need to think about what's best for me, and you need to do the same thing."

"I have money. Plenty of money…wait here."

I ran out of the diner, grabbed my bag from the truck, and ran back inside. I dumped the bag out, and when the gold coins hit the table, everyone in the diner turned to look.

"Where did you get this?" Milly said.

"Rue said I'd need it, and she was right. There are thousands of dollars here. We could stay on the road for years. Forever. Drive up to Canada for the summer and then down south when it gets cold. We could visit every national and state park in the country. When we get tired of camping, we could stay in a motel for a few days. I've always wanted to see the Grand Canyon, Yosemite…I've never been to Florida, Maine, or the Great Lakes. This country is so big, they'll never find us, and when the war is over, they'll forget all about the bombing and the draft. We'll have different names by then, different lives…"

"Jim. Put the coins back in the bag."

"It's going to be ok," I said, my voice unsteady. "You got enough money in this country, you can get away with anything…and this is a lot of money."

"Put the coins away…now."

I scooped up the coins and shoved them in the bag.

The waitress came to the table, and Milly ordered coffee and an omelet. We were quiet, looking out the window at the mountains. I could feel myself losing control, and for the first time, I saw myself as Milly saw me. A young, scared kid with no skills, running from the law.

"We need to find a place where we can hide for a few months," she said. "A cabin somewhere out there." She waved her hand at the window. "Lay low for the summer. I've been in overdrive for the past four years, Jim. I need to stop moving for a while. The road is killing me. I can't do it anymore."

Milly paid for the meals, and we turned to walk out. Next to the cash register was a community bulletin board with handwritten notices pinned to it. Ads for home cleaning services, hairdressers, snowplowing, landscaping, and a cabin for rent. I pulled the ad for the cabin off the board and stuffed it in my pocket.

39

We took Highway 21 north out of Stanley for a few miles, then turned on a dirt road that climbed up and over a low hill and down into a wide valley at the foot of a steep ridge. A narrow stream, full of melting snow, rushed along the edge of the road. The woman from the ad said we'd see two large boulders marking the start of the driveway leading up to the cabin. I thought we'd gone too far when we saw the boulders, as big as cars. One on either side of the rutted gravel road.

The truck bounced up the rough driveway through a dense stand of trees until we saw a small wooden cabin in a clearing. A thin sheet of snow covered the roof. Ice was banked up in the shadows under the trees. The house had a rock chimney, a small screened-in porch, and a tall stack of firewood in the yard. The key was under a rock by the door.

The place was small and dusty. The woman said she hadn't rented the cabin in years. There was a big living room with a kitchen on one side, a large fireplace, two tiny bedrooms, and a bathroom. The only heat was the fireplace. A layer of dust covered the worn-out furniture.

We dragged the sofa and beds out into the sun and spent the day sweeping and cleaning. It was close to sundown when we got everything back in the house. I started a fire, and after a while, the place got so warm I had to open the windows. The tiny stove actually worked. Milly baked a chicken and potatoes, and we sat in front of the fire, eating our dinner, watching the sun go down through dirty windows.

40

In a few weeks, most of the snow was gone. We started taking walks along the road, up toward the mountains. The land was thick with running creeks. Muddy trails cut through the dense woods and around the lakes. We saw a few people on our walks until one afternoon, a woman driving a beat-up station wagon stopped us and asked if we were renting the Zimmer place. Milly told her we had the place until September or the first snow.

"That could be any day," the woman said. "I've seen snow fall on the Fourth of July."

She invited us up to her place for a drink. "Ignore my dog," she said. "She barks something terrible, but she's friendly."

Her name was Libby. She was a nurse in the clinic in Ketchum. Five days a week, she made the hour-long trip down the mountain to work. She loved the isolation of living in the woods, no people around, just her and the dog.

"It's not that I don't like people," she said, "I just don't trust most of them."

We were sitting outside Libby's cabin, drinking wine one afternoon. Milly and Libby were talking, and I was throwing a stick for the dog.

"How long have you lived up here?" Milly said.

"Three years. Moved here from California…to get away from my former life."

"What were you running away from?" Milly said.

"It's a long story."

"We've got lots of wine…"

Libby smiled. "I'm not running away from anything. I prefer to imagine myself moving toward a better life. I took a lot of acid back in LA. We were all looking for enlightenment. Sitting around at the beach waiting for God to speak to us. All I got was this weird buzzing in my ears. Maybe it was God's dial tone. Or his busy signal.

"The only thing the drugs did was intensify my mental issues. Eventually, I went to see a shrink. Nice guy, had a lot of insight into my problems. I liked him until he tried to get me into bed. Said what I needed was some restorative sex, and he was volunteering. I asked him if all his patients needed a sex cure or if it was only the young women.

"I was grateful for one thing he told me. He said I should walk for thirty minutes a day. Said it would help clear my head. He was right. I started walking, then I started running. Felt better almost overnight, lost some weight, slept better. Every morning, I'd get up early and run from my house up in Laurel Canyon down the hill and back. Five miles a day.

"I was living with this guy who was trying to be an actor. Really, what he was doing was living off me. I was paying the rent, and all he did was go to a few auditions, then come home and smoke weed all afternoon. After I started running, I began to see my life for what it was. Empty, a complete waste. I was living off my parents' money, waiting for them to die so I could inherit even more money and move up to an expensive house in Brentwood, where my decadent lifestyle could reach new levels of depravity. So I threw my loser boyfriend out of the house and tried to start over.

"One day I was running along the road, and I stepped in a hole, twisted my ankle. The pain was intense. So I'm hobbling along the road trying to get home, and a car pulls up and stops. A young girl about my age asks if I need help. She looked harmless, so I got in. She was a nurse. Took one look at my ankle and told me I should get it X-rayed. We started talking about her job. She worked in the ER. Every day was different, she said, you didn't know who would walk in the door. Something clicked, I don't know. It was her attitude, her competence. I asked for her number. I wanted to know more about nursing. We became friends, and eventually I enrolled in nursing school. The courses were hard, especially after blowing off most of my education. But I graduated and got a job."

Libby sat back in her chair.

"More wine?" Milly said.

"Yes, please." Milly filled her glass.

"Everything was going great. New job, new apartment.
And then I was kidnapped."

"What?"

"My loser ex-boyfriend knew how much money my family had, how much I'd inherited. And he wanted some of it."

"What happened?"

"I'm walking up the stairs to my apartment, and this guy shoves a gun in my back, tells me not to turn around. They put me in the trunk of a car and drove out to the desert to some shack. They tie me to a chair and put a bag over my head. I can hear them talking in the next room. Art wants this. Art wants that. Art was my ex. So I knew he was behind it. I tried to stay cool. I was sure my parents would pay the ransom, and I'd be released in a few days." Libby took a drink.

"I was out there, tied up with a bag over my head for seven days. I started to lose it. Some guy would come into the room and slap me around, tell me he was going to rape me, cut my throat, and bury me in the desert. I started hallucinating. I thought I'd already died and this was my punishment."

Libby took a deep breath. "Haven't talked about this in a while…"

"You don't have to say any more…" Milly said.

"No, no…I'm fine. Ancient history. Turned out almost no one knew I was missing. When I didn't show up for work, my supervisor called my apartment, but that was the only person who knew I was gone. I wasn't talking to my parents, and my old friends weren't in touch that often. Kinda sad...I get kidnapped, and nobody notices."

"The kidnappers got bored after a week and drove me back to my apartment. The whole thing did something to my head. I got very paranoid and couldn't sleep. I was always checking the doors and windows. I was a mess. Then I saw an ad for a nurse in Ketchum. I looked it up on a map. Small town in rural Idaho, it sounded perfect. So here I am. I don't know how long I'll stay here, but I know I'll never go back to LA."

"Don't you get lonely...up here by yourself?" Milly said.

"Are you asking me about my sex life?"

"No, I just..." Libby laughed. "I have a friend in Ketchum. A few times a month, we have a sleepover."

41

The days were getting warmer, and the snow melted from under the trees. County maintenance crews began to fill all the potholes on our road. There were more birds around: crows, blackbirds, magpies.

I was in the kitchen making a sandwich when Milly walked in the door and sat down at the table.

"I'm pregnant."

I was shocked but not surprised. I'd just assumed she was on the pill or taking precautions or something.

"Are you sure?"

"Yes, I'm sure."

"What are you gonna do?"

"I'm still trying to get my head around it."

I knew I shouldn't have said it, but I did anyway. "Who do you think the father is?"

She glared at me. "Fuck off. Not you, that's for sure." She went to her room and slammed the door.

I took my sandwich outside and sat for a long time, watching the sun sink behind the mountains. The sky turned this beautiful yellowish-pink, and the air got cold.

A flock of birds flew over the house, tiny black wedges against the fading light. If only my life were that easy, a graceful separation from the earth and off into the sky.

A few days later, we were up at Libby's. Milly was grilling hamburgers. Libby and I were playing cards, using an upturned bucket for a table.

Libby looked up at Milly. "If you know who the father is, you might want to let him know."

Milly laughed. "Could be anybody. Could be a kid in New Orleans, might be a saxophone player from Louisiana, or a drug dealer in Austin. No, that's too far back. Might be a jailbird from LA."

Or a redneck cop from Montana, I thought.

"Wow," Libby said. "You've had a lot of fun."

Milly smiled. "Yeah, I have. But I'm giving up men for a while. Apparently, I can't be trusted around them."

"What about Jim?" Libby said. "Is he on the list?"

"Jim?...no. He's just my faithful platonic sidekick."

42

I decided to go see Nancy in California. I knew it was risky, but I wanted to see if she was ok. See if there was anything left of my family. And I wanted to get away from Milly for a while, try to figure out how I felt about her. I wasn't abandoning her; Libby was close by if she needed anything.

My plan was to drive down to LA, stay a few days, then drive up the coast and eventually back to Idaho. Or maybe keep going up into Canada and then Alaska. I felt safer on the road, constantly moving. I was wanted by the state of Montana as well as the United States government. Maybe I was fooling myself, but I thought if I never slowed down, never stayed in one place too long, I'd be harder to find.

When I told Milly about my plans, she looked relieved.

I left early one morning in late June. I stopped for gas in Boise and then headed south. The sky was empty, the highway was empty. Vast fields of sage with dry grass growing up to the edge of the road and in the distance, rocky, barren hills. Nothing to look at, nothing on the radio. The drive was so monotonous, I had to stop a few times, climb out of the truck, and shake myself awake.

I arrived in LA just in time for rush hour. I drove to Santa Monica, parked by the beach, and walked along the boardwalk until I found a phone booth. All I had was a phone number, no address. I dialed the number and waited.

After several rings, a man's voice said, "Hello."

"Yeah…I'm looking for Nancy Birdwell."

"She's not here right now…who's this?"

"Uh…a friend from back home."

"She won't be home until later. Call back, or I can take a message."

"Mind if I come over and wait for her. I'm not really a friend, I'm her brother."

Silence and then, "Yeah, I guess."

She lived in Silver Lake in an upstairs apartment. It was dark when I got there. I parked the truck, locked it, and walked up the stairs. I knocked and waited. The door was opened by a young guy with sunglasses and no shirt, hair down to his shoulders. He didn't say anything, just stood in the doorway.

"I'm Jim."

"Yeah…come on in." He stepped aside.

"You hungry? I was just going to roll one and make a smoothie."

"I could eat, I guess."

He stood at the kitchen counter rolling a joint. "If you left anything in your car, man, I'd bring it inside. Neighborhood's kinda sketchy."

He lit the joint and smoked most of it before offering it to me. Then he set a record on a turntable, put on headphones, and stretched out on the sofa. "Nancy should be home in a few hours."

I still didn't know his name.

When Nancy walked in the door, she put down her bag and ran over to hug me. It was the best I'd felt in a long time. My sister's arms are around me. Maybe there was something left of my messed-up family.

I stood at the counter while she scrambled eggs and told me about her new life. They'd driven straight to California, she and Gary. He got a job at an auto repair shop, and she found work trying to sell real estate over the phone. Hated it, she said. They broke up. Not a big deal, she shrugged. After that, a series of fast food jobs, then parking cars, and finally as a waitress at a restaurant on Melrose.

"It's cool," she said. "Some of the customers are on TV.
Tips are great."

"Who's the guy on the sofa?"

"That's Reece."

"Is he your boyfriend?"

"No way. He works in the movie business. Gaffer, grip…I don't know."

We stepped out on a tiny balcony into the warm air. The glow from millions of cars, houses, and buildings lit up the night. The constant buzz of traffic. A plane glided overhead, lights blinking. She put her hand on my shoulder.

"Mom told me about the draft. What are you going to do?"

"I'm not going. Don't care what the old man says. This is my life, I'm not gonna waste it."

She nodded. "You're welcome to stay as long as you want."

43

The next day, I drove to Santa Monica, sat by the boardwalk, and watched the crowds. Everyone was on the move, walking, jogging, and skateboarding. I felt like I was stuck. I knew I could stay in LA and find a job. It was a big city, and it would be easy to hide with so many people around. But something didn't feel right. Crowds made me a little anxious. The traffic, the noise, the smog.

For the past few months, I had been in constant motion, across the South, into Texas, through the West, and up into Idaho. Maybe the best thing to do would be to head back to Stanley when the baby arrived. Milly might need me. Or not. She was the least dependent person I'd ever met.

I walked along the boardwalk and up to Ocean Boulevard. Barefoot girls in bikinis drifting down the sidewalk. A blond kid on a skateboard weaved around an older couple. I moved past the pier and the Ferris wheel. A guy in a convertible at a stoplight was yelling at a crowd of girls standing on the corner.

I crossed the street and stepped into a pawn shop, just to look around. In a glass case at the back of the store was a shelf of cameras. The owner was asking twenty bucks for a used Polaroid. I offered him ten and walked out the door with it.

After a few days, Nancy's apartment seemed to get a lot smaller. Reece was between jobs, so he was lying around all day. And Nancy was at the restaurant until late at night. I decided to leave LA. I wasn't going anywhere as much as I was getting away from something. I thought if I could stay mobile, maybe I could stay free.

I took the Pacific Coast Highway north. The winding road hugged the coast for hundreds of miles. This was the extreme left edge of America, an endless blue ocean rolling in on the sand. The clouds that morning looked like a fleet of white boats streaming across the sky. Sleek, smooth, ovalshaped.

I stopped for gas in Naples, filled the tank, and went inside to pay. When I came out, a young girl was standing by the truck. She looked up as I walked over. "Is this your truck?" I nodded.

"Are you headed north?"

"Not sure where I'm going."

She was young, high school age maybe, with long black hair that fell across one eye.

"You don't know where you're going?"

"Nope." I opened the door and slid behind the wheel.

"I need a ride, I'll give you gas money."

"How old are you?"

She made a face. "Old enough."

"Is anyone looking for you? Parents? Boyfriend?"

She pushed her hair behind her ear. "That's not really any of your business…is it?"

"I guess not. Hop in."

We stayed on Highway 1 up through Lompoc, Santa Maria, and Pismo Beach. She was quiet, leaning against the door, watching the ocean roll by. All I'd had for breakfast was coffee, and now, in the late afternoon, I was starving. I pulled into a burger place in Morro Bay, got out, and stretched. She stayed in the car.

"Are you hungry?" I said.

"I don't have any money."

"Don't worry about it. I got

it." She looked at me

suspiciously.

"It's ok," I said. "It's just lunch."

We sat outside at a picnic table with milkshakes and fries, watching boats moving around in the bay. The sun was bright, and the flat, blue water didn't look real. She seemed to relax a little.

"Where do you live?" I said.

"Ventura."

"What's it like?"

"Small town, nothing there really. Nothing for me anyway."

"Where are you headed?"

She put her hands on the table and looked at me. "I'm not going anywhere. I'm just going."

"Sounds like my life. The Army drafted me, but I'm not going."

"So you're a draft dodger," she said.

"I guess. What are you dodging?"

She ran her hand through her hair. "Mom has a new boyfriend, and he can't decide who he likes better, her or me."

I didn't know what to say. We sat watching the ocean, the warm sun on our faces.

I put out my hand. "My name is Jim."

She shook my hand and said, "Amy."

Back in the truck, back on the highway.

"There's a map in the glovebox," I said.

She snapped it open. "What's this?" She held up Milly's gun.

"Just put that under the seat."

"Why do you have a gun?"

"I don't know…protection?"

She shoved it under the seat and opened the map.

"You're the one who needs protection," I said,

"hitchhiking by yourself."

"I'm careful. If I get a bad vibe from someone, I don't get in the car."

"Will your Mom call the cops or anything when you don't come home?"

"I doubt it. Her new guy takes up all her time. He's very spiritual. Loves Elvis, Jesus, and money. In that order. He's a psycho, but my mom can't see it because she's in love." She looked out the window. "If that's love, count me out."

"Everyone is confused these days," I said. "The war, the riots, astronauts lost in space. The only thing that makes sense to me is to keep moving."

She nodded. "It's like every absurd weirdo nowadays has his own devoted following."

"People want to believe in something," I said. "Even if it's crazy."

"Or maybe they're just lazy. It's dangerous to let someone else do your thinking for you."

She was quiet and then said, "We need a king or an emperor or something. This country's too dumb for democracy."

44

We drove past Santa Cruz, went around San Francisco, and up through Point Reyes. She held the map in her lap all afternoon, calling out the little towns, local landmarks, and public beaches we passed through. By late afternoon, we were in Mendocino. I was tired and hungry. She looked at the map and found a state park where we could camp.

The park was empty. A thin dark river flowed out of the low hills, cut through the beach, and emptied into the ocean. I set up the tent on the sand and threw my sleeping bag inside. We walked into Mendocino and bought hot dogs, potato chips, and marshmallows, and, after lying about my age, a six-pack of Pacifico.

We walked along the empty beach until we'd collected enough driftwood for a big fire. Stacking the wood in a rough pyramid, I lit it up, and we watched the bright flames flail in the breeze. I opened a beer, handed it to her, and got one for myself. We were quiet, standing by the fire, mesmerized by the heat and light. She seemed to be thinking about something or on the verge of speaking. But mostly she was quiet.

The fire burned down to glowing embers, and we roasted the hot dogs on sticks. The ocean was out there somewhere in the dark, hissing loudly, waves falling on the sand.

I offered to share the tent with her, but she said she'd prefer the truck. I gave her some of my clothes to roll up for a pillow, and she climbed into the truck.

The next morning, we stopped for coffee in Mendocino and got back on the highway, heading north. The day was warm, with a bright sky and thin white clouds hanging over the blue water. Amy studied the map all morning.

My camera was on the seat between us. She picked it up. "What's that for?" I shrugged.

She pointed it at me and pushed the button. The picture slid out of the camera.

"Having any second thoughts about running away?" I said.

"Usually, I just cruise up the coast for a few hours and then go back home. But this seems kinda like an adventure."

"Where would you like to go?"

She put a finger on the map. "Here. The giant redwoods."

A few hours later, we were in a forest, walking along a wide trail at the foot of the largest trees in the world. Towering wooden pillars with green branches hundreds of feet above our heads. The tops of the red giants were hidden in the mist, each tree wider and taller than the next.

Amy ran ahead, deeper into the woods. I couldn't see her and called her name.

"Over here," she yelled.

She was lying on her back, looking up at the distant canopies vanishing in clouds.

"This is how to enjoy the trees," she said.

I lay down beside her and looked up. It was overwhelming. The massive red trunks, living things as tall as skyscrapers. She grabbed my hand, rolled on top of me, and began to kiss me. The flesh of my mouth came alive. I felt dizzy.

It didn't last long. She stood up, brushed herself off, and walked away.

When I got back to the truck, she was sitting in the front seat looking at the map.

"Where to now?" I said.

"Crater Lake. The deepest lake in the country."

"That was nice," I said.

She looked up from the map. "My mom is always telling me to get in touch with my emotions. But I don't put a lot of faith in feelings. They come, and they go. Clouds block the sun, and it gets dark. The clouds move on, it's sunny again. That's how much you can count on emotions. I'll settle for getting in touch with my mind."

We got back on the highway, and the sky went dark; gray clouds rolled in, low over the trees. A steady downpour began to flood the pavement, and waves of water rolled across the highway. I parked under an overpass to wait out the storm. Amy had fallen asleep against the door. I watched the rain, bouncing on the asphalt. What if a cop stopped us and found out she was an underage runaway? I'd be arrested for kidnapping. Maybe I should give her some money and let her bus it home? Or has she decided to be my permanent traveling companion?

I got out of the truck to check my bag, and the coins were still there. When I climbed back in, Amy was holding the pistol.

"You should put that away. It's dangerous."

"I'm taking the truck," she said softly.

"What?"

"I'm taking the truck. I want you to get out."

"You don't even have a driver's license."

"I have my learner's permit, I'll be fine."

"I thought there was something between us."

She shook her head. "The only thing between us is this gun."

I climbed out and grabbed my bag. I watched the truck accelerate onto the wet highway and disappear into the trees. I stood there for a long time, certain she'd change her mind and come back for me. After a while, the clouds lifted, and the rain stopped. I walked to the edge of the highway and stuck out my thumb.

www.ingramcontent.com/pod-product-compliance
Lightning Source LLC
Chambersburg PA
CBHW071541030726
47598CB00001B/188